SOUP & ME

SOUP, Robert Newton Peck's lighthearted stories about his boyhood friend, recreated the good times the two had growing up in a small Vermont town earlier in the century. Now, Soup is back again, getting himself and his best pal Rob into more and better mischief.

From the crisp Vermont spring to the chill of winter, Soup and Rob learn, among other things, not to leave their clothes on the bank of the creek when Janice Riker is around; find Soup's tonsorial talents leave a lot to be desired; chase a runaway pumpkin down Sutter's hill; blaze a trail through Mrs. Stetson's marigolds; have a fight with a turkey; and provide Miss Kelly with a Christmas she'll never forget.

These are lively and heartwarming stories reflecting a gentler time, but the shared adventures of a boy and his friend are as new as today.

BOOKS BY ROBERT NEWTON PECK

SOUP *&* ME

ROBERT NEWTON PECK

ILLUSTRATED BY CHARLES LILLY

Alfred A. Knopf New York

Many thanks to Selden and Susie and Laura, three friends without whose help this book would have been unreadable, and to Marghan Miller who thought of the title.

R. N. P.

THIS IS A BORZOI BOOK PUBLISHED BY ALFRED A. KNOPF, INC.

Text Copyright © 1975 by Robert Newton Peck. Illustrations Copyright © 1975 by Alfred A. Knopf, Inc. All rights reserved under International and Pan-American Copyright Conventions. Published in the United States by Alfred A. Knopf, Inc., New York, and simultaneously in Canada by Random House of Canada Limited, Toronto. Distributed by Random House, Inc., New York. Library of Congress Cataloging in Publication Data Peck, Robert Newton. Soup II. SUMMARY: The further adventures and misadventures of Rob and Soup, two boys growing up in a small Vermont town. [1. Friendship–Fiction] I. Title.
PZ7.P339Sp [Fic] 75–9514
ISBN 0–394–83157–8
ISBN 0–394–93157–2 lib. bdg. Manufactured in the United States of America.
10

IN FOND MEMORY OF MISS KELLY.
WE WERE HER GARDEN,
HER FAMILY, AND HER LIFE.

Contents

SOUP & ME

1

Janice Riker Strikes Again

"Gee," said Soup. "Sure is hot."

"Yep," I said, "it sure is."

"And it's only the fifth of May."

Soup and I were taking the short cut home from school; the back way, through the south end of Mr. Fiddler's pasture. As we walked along the ridge, jumping from one big rock to another, we weren't in too much of a hurry.

"I guess that's why Miss Kelly let us go home early," I said.

"And if this hot spell keeps up," said Soup, "maybe we'll get out of school early every day."

"That would sure be swell."

"Sure would."

"Soup?"

"Yeah."

"Miss Kelly is a regular guy."

"Sometimes."

"Take today. She didn't *have* to let us go early, but she did."

"Heat probably got to her. I bet Miss Kelly's near to a hundred years old."

"Rolly McGraw said she's over eighty."

"How would he know?"

"He just knows," I said.

"No, he don't," said Soup. "Rolly McGraw is so dumb he'd have to take off his shoes and socks to count twenty."

"You mean to count his toes?" I said.

"Rolly's got ten toes, just like every other kid. Seven on his left foot and three on his right."

Soup and I got to laughing so hard we fell off a rock on purpose so's we could roll around on the sweet meadow grass that the cows kept short. My mind kept seeing seven toes on Rolly's foot (he really had five) and it was so doggone funny. We giggled on the ground until we were both a wash of sweat.

"Yikes, I'm hot," said Soup. He sprawled on his back.

"Me too."

"Let's shuck off our shoes and socks and walk barefoot."

"Okay by me."

It didn't take long to skin off our footwear. The grass was sort of a prickle feeling under my feet. Like each blade of grass whispered summer was coming.

"You got dirt between your toes," said Soup, pointing at my feet.

"So do you."

"My mother always says that, too."

Using our pointing fingers like a saw, we rubbed back and forth, each one of us working to clean the gaps between our toes. The black dirt came off in tiny rolls, like the modeling clay at school.

"Hey!" I said, taking a whiff on my finger. "My toes smell like vinegar."

"Huh," said Soup, smelling his own finger. "So do mine. Maybe we both need a bath."

"Maybe we do."

From up on the ridge we could look down and see the crick that ran through Mr. Fiddler's pasture and under the fence, flowing back toward town. Beyond the fence the houses were close together.

"Know where that water goes?" said Soup.

"Sure. Everybody knows that. It goes to fill up Putt's Pond."

"Rob?"

"Yeah."

"You ever wondered who Putt is? Or was?"

"Once I did. I reckon he was the guy who discovered Putt's Pond; or he owned it or something."

"Probably," said Soup.

"Maybe he was the first guy who took a swim in it."

"That crick water sure looks cool."

"It's only May. My mother says I can't go for a swim until June."

"My mother said the same thing," said Soup.

"So did Miss Kelly."

"I bet *she'd* know who Putt is."

"Miss Kelly knows everything," I said.

"Except for one," said Soup.

"What's that?"

"I'll wager," said Soup, "she doesn't know what it's like to take a swim in good old Putt's Pond."

"At least not in May," I said.

"Do you suppose Miss Kelly ever takes a swim?"

"She probably doesn't even own a bathing suit."

"Neither do you," said Soup. "And come to think of it, I don't either."

"Who needs a bathing suit?" I said.

"We don't," said Soup.

"Nope," I said. "Just girls do."

"You know, Rob . . . it wouldn't do us any hurt to walk down and *look* at the water."

"We wouldn't have to go in," I said.

"Unless we fell in," said Soup. I didn't like the way he said it. There was sort of a splash in his voice that was both wet and cold. Soup had pushed me into water of one body or another more than once. He pushed me into Fiddler's Crick, Lake Champlain, the mudhole near Mr. Tanner's barn, the sump at the stone quarry, and also into Atwood's Brook.

Soup had never pushed me into Putt's Pond, so I decided right then and there he wasn't going to. At least not today.

"Maybe we best go home," I said.

"Come on," he said. "All we'll do is just skip a few dumb old stones."

Down the hill we ran, dropping a shoe here and a sock there, stopping to scoop them up again. My bare toe got a good stub on a pebble that was half buried in the May mud, but it didn't hurt that much. We climbed the fence, walking behind a long row of houses until we got to our destiny.

Putt's Pond was full up.

Soup picked up a flat stone and made it sail across the silver surface toward the old millhouse. It waltzed along the water in a merry little dance, until it finally sank. I threw mine. But it didn't go as far as Soup's.

"Mine went farther," said Soup.

"I don't care," I said. Yet I threw my next rock so hard it made my shoulder ache.

Soup stuck his toe into the water and pulled it out again real quick. "Feels real great," he said.

I did it too. The water was quite a shock. Mountain cricks in May up in Vermont were never intended to swab the human body. I looked into the water to see if there were any chunks of ice still left. My toe was pink when I stuck it in, and white coming out.

"It's not so cold," I lied.

"Warm, I'd say. Let's go in. Aren't you sort of hot?"

"Not *that* hot."

"Come on, Rob! We'll just skin down, jump in, get right out again, and get ourselves dressed. It'll cool us off."

My toe stuck itself into the liquid ice of Putt's Pond, taking all the courage I could muster to hold its head under. Seeing as it was the toe that got stubbed, I figured the cold water might be good for what ailed it.

We snaked off all our clothes.

Standing in the water of Putt's Pond up to our knocking knees, I turned to Soup to comment on the temperature of the water. But my teeth were chattering a conversation of their own, like my mouth was talking to itself. Slowly, I felt the cold coming up my white legs. Earlier there had been a bit of Vermont topsoil between my toes. Smelly, but warm. But now there was mud between my toes, mud from the dark and murky bottom of Putt's Pond, mud that was still sleeping and a parcel of Vermont winter, not awake to the first warm day we'd had since late October.

My toes were in agony.

"It's not cold," said Soup. "Not to *me*."

"Me neither," I could barely say.

"What say we swim out to The Log and back." It was an old familiar log, half submerged into Putt's Pond since Miss Kelly herself was a mere tadpole. The Log wasn't anywhere near the shore.

"It looks kind of *far* out there," I said.

"You can swim," said Soup.

"I can *think*, too."

"About what?" Soup's voice was shaking.

"About freezing to death."

"You only freeze to death in the winter," said Soup, "and you have to be up north in the Yukon or someplace like that."

"How do you know?"

"I got a Jack London book. Honest."

"Well, if you ask me, Soup, even Jack London wouldn't swim all the way to The Log."

"Sure he would. Jack London is the greatest swimmer in the whole world. Everybody knows that. Jack could swim in a pond like this all day and call it lukewarm."

"What's *luke* mean?" I said.

"Something in the Bible. I think it means water."

Well, I guess Soup wouldn't hold me in high esteem if I was afraid of just a few buckets of cold luke. After all, it was a hot day.

"Okay," I said, "out to The Log and back."

In we went, head first. And for a moment, as we kicked underwater through the dark depths (we were at least three feet down, which is a respectable half a fathom), I thought my heart was going to stop. We made it to The Log. Panting and puffing, the two white and naked frogs pulled themselves up on the dry wood to sun themselves. And to get their blood going.

Soup and I looked at each other, icy water from our mops of hair cascading down our freckled faces, too frozen to even speak. Soup's mouth was open. He tried to say something, but the words wouldn't pass his purple lips. He shook like a rattle. So did I. But after ten minutes we were near to dry as we sat on The Log, trying to reason a route back to shore that did not entail an immersing into the inhospitable waters of Putt's Pond.

This was when we saw Janice Riker.

There had always been a dispute between Soup and me. When the subject came up as to who was the toughest kid in school, only two names were ever mentioned. Eddy Tacker was the school bully according to Soup. Yet compared to old Janice, I saw Eddy Tacker as practically being somewhere between Heidi and Rebecca of Sunnybrook Farm.

When we put on the school pageant, the one we did on famous people when each kid got to dress up as a celebrity, you should have seen Janice Riker in *her* costume. Soup was George Washington, and I was Calvin Coolidge who was our country's best president because he was from Vermont. Before the pageant, Soup and I had told Miss Kelly about two famous people we *really* wanted to be. But for some reason or other, known only to herself, Miss Kelly informed both Soup and me (using her patient and understanding voice) that it was her opinion that the honored halls of history would be best served if we were to choose two people other than Buck Jones and Tom Mix.

Miss Kelly, in fact, suggested that we be George Washington and Calvin Coolidge, even though we tried to tell her that neither one had ever been, to our knowledge, a cowboy in the movies. And it was also Miss Kelly who suggested famous people for some of our classmates to dress up as. Eddy Tacker wanted to be Bulldog Drummond, but he had to be content with just Herod the King.

Janice Riker got to be Lucretia Borgia.

At the time, nobody seemed to recall that much about Mrs. Borgia or what she was so famous for. All I know is that Miss Kelly sort of got a kick out of the whole idea. Not that she laughed or anything like that. Yet she seemed to assume a more gay disposition than usual. I even asked her if she was a bit giddy and felt all right.

"Yes," she said, "I'm just in an expansive mood."

I asked Soup what expansive meant, and he cleared up matters by telling me that it cost a lot of money. Which made me wonder as to who was planning to buy Miss Kelly.

"Hey," Soup said, "there's Janice."

"Boy, do I hate that girl," I said. Soup and I hid parts of our bodies behind The Log for modesty's sake.

"Who doesn't," said Soup. He stuck out his tongue.

"I hope when she grows up she marries Eddy Tacker."

"Yeah," said Soup, "but let's hope they don't have any kids. It'd be a sorry shame if those two ever had a litter of ten."

"Sure would. It would be like coming across ten roaches under your sink," I said.

"You'd want to spray 'em with Flit."

"Hope she doesn't see us," I said.

Janice saw us. As we sat out on The Log, I suddenly knew Janice Riker had spotted us when I saw her bend over to pick up a rock. She threw it at us.

Plunk!

The stone made a splash far short of its target, which was either Soup's head or mine. Even from our dry perch away out in the center of the pond, we could read the disappointment on Janice Riker's face. Her miss made her heartsick. It got me to sort of wondering if Lucretia Borgia had ever throwed a stone across Putt's Pond. Halfway across, I was thinking as Janice bent to select her next missile, would be more than enough to hit us. Again she threw.

Plunk!

Janice was the undisputed queen of our school when it came to just plain being ornery. But she was no scholar. Brawny she was. But when the brains were handed out, it must have been the one day in her life that she went placidly to the end of the line, a courtesy she rarely extended at the drinking fountain. She threw rock after rock. None reached us. And the angrier Janice Riker became, the bigger the rocks she selected. Smaller ones might have reached us, but such logic escaped her thoughts. In fact, one rock that she attempted to hurl in our direction was bigger than her head (and probably more intelligent). Its trajectory was a brief but graceless arc which ended abruptly on the instep of her front foot (Janice threw in the style of a shotputter), causing her to howl like a heifer.

We laughed. Janice searched for a rock that was bigger still.

It's no easy feat to throw a rock so big that you can't even lift it off the ground. Only somebody with no brains at all would try. Janice tried it. Bending low and grunting like a gorilla, she showed little progress on altering the rock's location. But she showed us far more than just a glimpse of raw determination. She showed us her panties.

That's not quite correct, because she wasn't wearing any. What she showed us, to be perfectly honest, was the place where panties should have been. Soup and I laughed so hard we had to hang on to each other or we'd have fallen in the drink.

"Yah! Yah! Yah!" yelled Soup in a jeer.

"Ha! Ha! Can't hit us," I hollered.

"Nyah! Nyah! Janice," we chanted over and over again, as the pantless pitcher tossed rock after rock, each falling far short of The Log. But all of the sudden our laughter came to an abrupt and quiet halt. Silence was once again restored to the sunny shores of Putt's Pond, as the two of us saw the object in Janice Riker's fist that she surely intended to be her very next waterbound missile.

It was Soup's shoe.

Plunk!

Bubbles rose as it sank slowly to what we knew might well be its eternal rest in the waters of Putt. Before we could recover from the shock, its mate joined it, less than a full splash away. Janice must have thought it would have been a shame to break up the pair. My shoes went next. And then one of Soup's socks, with a pebble in it to make it really sail.

"She can't do that," said Soup.

"She's doing it," I said.

Three more socks went into the air and into Putt's Pond. And then Soup's pants, my pants and shirt, Soup's shirt and somebody's underwear. At so great a distance, and with tears starting to fill our eyes, it was difficult to determine whether it was Soup's undershorts or mine, as that particular article of unidentified clothing took a dive. Now in Janice's hand was the one remaining of all the bits of clothing. It was a pair of white undershorts.

Stepping into them with surprising agility, Janice hauled them up over her previously unclad loins. A tight fit. Thus our tormentor tossed us a final farewell and waddled off, underwear and all.

"What'll we do, Soup?"

"Get wet," Soup said.

For some reason the water seemed to be ten times colder during our swim to shore. My heart was hitting me with hammer blows. I thought we'd never make it, but finally our feet touched the deadly cold mud of Putt's Pond's bottom. My own bottom was equally cold; and from what I could observe, so was Soup's.

I found one of my shoes, bobbing sole up in the dark water near the shore, apparently with enough air inside it to keep it partially afloat. I put it on and tied it. But there's something about being dressed in one soppy wet shoe that still gives you the feeling of being near to nudity. One shoe doesn't cover up a whole lot. Soup found a sock, but that was all. We looked, but no more of our wardrobe was available.

Except for my shoe and Soup's sock, we were dripping wet, shivering cold, stark naked, and over a mile from home. Other than those minor discomforts, it had been a peachy afternoon.

"How'll we get home, Soup?"

"Walk, I reckon."

"What are you going to tell your mother?"

"Haven't figured that out yet. We may never *get* home, so why worry about that now."

"Which way'll we go?" I said.

"We can't go the way we come. Too many houses. Maybe it's even shorter if we go crosslots and cut behind the Baptist church."

"Okay by me," I said, "as long as I get home by chore time."

"Here we go," said Soup.

Leaving the pond, we sneaked along a hedge between two houses and then ran down First Street as fast as one shoe and one sock would carry us. Darting beside Rooker's Garage, we ended up breathless in a patch of shrubbery near the back of the Baptist church.

We heard voices.

"Who's that, Soup?"

"Some ladies."

"What are they doing?"

"Talking. What else? I can see 'em. They're toting some boxes into the back door of the church."

"Boxes of what?"

"Clothes."

What a beautiful word, I thought. Clothes. Straining my neck, I could see a lady carrying a box. What a good person, I thought. What a kindly spirit.

The ladies talked for a long time. We crept close enough, inside the shrubbery, which had at least a million thorns, to hear every sentence. They talked about the hot weather and said the same things over and over until I never thought they'd stop. But finally they did, leaving and *locking* the church's back door. They left, and we tested the knob. Locked! Then, with Soup up on my shoulders, he tried a window. Seconds later we were inside the Baptist church, which was as still as a tomb. I felt like a ghost.

"It's like stealing from God," I said.

"Not really, Rob."

"I suppose it's our only real hope."

"This stuff seems to be for big people," said Soup, trying on a skirt that would have fit Miss Boland, our enormous school nurse. All the clothes in the world wouldn't cover Miss Boland, except for the garment

Soup carefully refolded and replaced inside the box.

"Here's a dress," I said, "with dots on it."

"Does it fit?" Soup asked.

"I can't walk around in a *dress*."

"You sure can't walk around without it," said Soup.

"It fits. Are you wearing a dress, too?"

"That's all there is. Just stuff for ladies. Aren't there any poor *men* in the world?"

"Any shoes?"

"Yes, but with high heels. This lady sure had big feet. Or short skis."

"How does your dress fit now?" I asked.

"Better. I tied a few knots in the belt. Some of the Baptist ladies in this town ought to cut down on short-cake."

"I'm ready. You?"

"Ready as I'll ever be," said Soup, "in a pink dress with yellow flowers on it."

"Mine's at least polka dot," I said.

Out we walked, and through town. It wasn't a short cut, but the longest trip home I ever took. Feet weren't made to walk on one shoe or one sock. More than one person stared at us. Their mouths popped open, but nobody said a word. I turned up my polka dot collar.

We got home.

How, I'll never know, but we made it to my front door.

Aunt Carrie took one look at us, and there was a big discussion (as Mrs. Vinson, Soup's mother was there at the time) as to where our clothes were. So we told the truth. No fib could ever have been as wild. We both got one whale of a licking for going swimming in May, losing our clothes, and sneaking in to rob the Baptists.

The next day at school I saw my undershorts, just after Janice Riker dropped her pencil.

2

Miss Boland's Victrola

"Rob?"

Even though my head was bent low over a drinking fountain (the only one in the school), I didn't have to straighten up to know *that* voice. It jingled like a silver bell, with a tiny tinkling quality that no other larynx could, as far as my trained ear would perceive, ever possess.

Norma Jean Bissell spoke my name.

Ah! The millions upon billions of times my heart had spoken hers. Norma Jean Bissell. And each time I heard her name in the solitude of my own silence, the Biss of Bissell became either Bliss or Kiss. Gulping just fast enough to almost drown, I turned away from the pleasures of slurping up the educational waters of Vermont, and there she was. I had failed to swallow all of my drink in one gulp, so half of it ran down my chin. Choking and coughing, I sprayed drops on the front of her dress. She smiled. I melted. The load of liquid inside my gullet began to simmer.

"There's going to be a dance," she said softly.

"A dance?"

"Yes. I heard Miss Kelly tell Miss Boland, the nurse. Boys have to dance with girls."

"Oh yeah?" I was a regular fireball at conversation.

"And I don't want Eddy Tacker or Rolly or Ally Tidwell to ask me," she said.

"Who *do* you want?" I said, hoping my voice wasn't shaking. The water I had managed to gag down had somehow sloshed into my knees. It was a weak feeling, sort of like a newborn calf trying to stand up for the first time.

"Guess," said Norma Jean Bissell, her voice steady as a beam in a barn.

"Soup?" I asked her, my soul about to shatter.

"Almost."

"Me?"

"Yes. Please ask me. Miss Kelly is going to tell us all about it soon. So if those other boys ask me, I'll say you asked first."

"Okay," I said.

"You will?"

"Sure."

"But you have to be my partner."

"I can't dance," I said to Norma Jean Bissell.

"I know. Neither can I, but Miss Boland is going to teach us all. Don't forget, Rob. Promise?"

"I promise."

As she turned to run into the room (the drinking fountain was sort of in what you might call a hall), my heart pounded . . . Norma . . . Jean . . . Bissell. So loud that I was scared the whole school would hear, as if an aviator flew over the whole doggone town and wrote some skywriting in lines of smoke that would never blow away, and it read: Robert Newton Peck loves Norma Jean Bissell. Aflame with desire, I took an extra gulp of water.

We all took our seats. From the corner of my eye, I admired Norma Jean Bissell and the almost princess-like grace of her hand as she picked her nose.

"Today," said Miss Kelly, "I have an announcement to make." I yawned. But as Miss Kelly's piercing look stabbed halfway down my throat, my hand shot up to cover the cavern of my indifference. "Today is the tenth of May. And exactly one month from today, on the tenth day of June, our school will hold its first Spring Dance."

Soup made his favorite disgusting noise, not loud enough, however, for any of Miss Kelly's fourteen ears to detect.

"*All* of you," said Miss Kelly, "shall participate in what we hope shall be a traditional as well as annual event. It should also be fun."

We heard a long blast of a car horn. We waited, as the

horn sounded as if it was stuck forever. Finally it stopped.

As all heads turned, including Miss Kelly's, into our classroom staggered a very enormous object. It was brown, wooden, shiny, in the shape of a giant box with a horn on top and a crank on the side. Hands held it with great care, as chubby legs in white stockings bore it closer and closer, depositing the giant object on Miss Kelly's desk. As the hands relaxed their grip, we could see that the white-clad porter was none other than Miss Boland, our school nurse. Actually, she was the County Nurse and visited our rural school once or twice a month, depending on the weather and how well her car would start.

Miss Boland was a very very very big lady, who drove a very very very small car, which she called a coop. Her coop was barely big enough for Miss Boland. I'll never know how she ever got herself and the big box into that car without a shoehorn or out without a crowbar.

Exhausted, poor Miss Boland slumped weakly into Miss Kelly's chair. As her heavy hips filled the furniture, one of the spindles underneath an armrest popped partly out. The rest of the chair, although weakened, held its line. The four legs creaked like wharf ropes. We all held our breath, hoping real hard that the old chair would give way, but somehow it held together. Miss Kelly appeared not to notice.

"Miss Boland," she announced, "has been kind enough to help us prepare for our forthcoming Spring Dance

and has consented to lend us the use of one of her most
valued possessions."

"It's a Victrola," wheezed Miss Boland, pointing at
the thing she'd lugged in.

"Yes, a Victrola," said Miss Kelly. "Can anyone in
the class tell us what service it performs?"

Yanking a finger from a nostril so quickly that it
almost popped like a cork, Norma Jean Bissell raised her
hand. "It plays music," said the silver bells. My heart
twanged like a banjo on Saturday night.

"Looks more like a coffin to me," whispered Soup.

"Yeah, for an elephant. Or maybe Miss Boland," I
whispered back, nearly destroying Soup with my wit.

"And," said Miss Kelly, "we will *all quietly listen,*
while Miss Boland lets us hear one of her favorite re-
cordings. You may all come forward to get a better
look."

With a stately nod of her head, Miss Kelly indicated
to Miss Boland that the stage was hers. It took even more
effort for Miss Boland to pry herself *out* of the chair.
Now totally detached at both ends, the loose spindle
clattered to the floor, rolled, and came to rest. Every
kid watched it, thinking the same thought. That poor
chair!

Many was the wintery occasion we'd all seen our
mammoth Miss Boland (cozily clad in a plaid mackinaw
that would have blanketed a Clydesdale stallion) bending over in front of her car to man the crank. A single
twist of her brawny arm seemed to almost lift the coop

up off its front wheels. She shook it like a dog does a
bone. One cold day in February, the coop had not
started. No amount of Miss Boland's great looping
cranks would persuade it to respond. Drawing back a
boot the size of a coal scuttle, Miss Boland presented the
coop with such a prodigious kick that it not only started,
it rolled backward for nearly thirty feet.

Miss Boland operated a Victrola with an attitude she
shared with all motor vehicles. It was woman against
contraption. The Victrola was more than chattel; it was
an adversary, worthy of what little Miss Boland apparently knew of either machinery or music. Bracing her
feet, and with a gesture that could have been a spit on
her hands, Miss Boland closed in on the helpless—but
we hoped a stubborn—Victrola. Miss Boland drew first
blood with a headlock, lifting up the stuck lid. She removed the silver Z, and with a small pause of difficulty,
managed to jab it into the flank of the wooden box.

Soup whispered, "Score one for Miss Boland."

It was a familiar scene, as Miss Boland cranked up the
Victrola in the manner she'd turn the crank of her car.
Around and around went her arm of iron and the silver
handle. It didn't sound much like music, but she did
look a bit like an organ grinder without a monkey. For
her, a gorilla.

"What's she doing?" Soup said.

I said "Making ice cream."

"To get that doo-hinky to play, I guess you gotta
twist its arm," said Soup.

Beneath the turntable was a cabinet, the doors of which Miss Boland now majestically opened as though they led to a throne room. Pulling out an enormous black disc that could have made a lid for a manhole, Miss Boland drew in a great breath to blow off the dust. Squinting, she read the small red spot in the center of the disc, through which was a tiny hole.

" 'Just a Song at Twilight,' " said Miss Boland, "and sung by a truly great Irish artist, Chauncey Olcott."

"Chauncey?" said Soup. "We're really in for it."

In the center of the round turntable was a shaft of silver that stuck straight up like a shiny little sentry. Its head was apparently intended to fit into the tiny hole in the center of the big black disc. But, as Miss Boland seemed to be on the verge of pointing out, the shaft was too large. Or the hole too diminutive. Bending her head low, and sighting down through the hole as she squinted one eye, Miss Boland (stalking it like a hungry cat) suddenly pounced the disc around its fitting, the silver shaft jabbing up through the hole and nearly up Miss Boland's nose.

"Score one for the Victrola," said Soup.

"I'm ready," said Miss Boland. "Children, you are in for a musical treat. This is my very *favorite* record." She pointed to the black disc.

Turning to her instrument with a gay flourish of her pudgy hand, she threw the switch. Nothing happened. Quickly, she reversed the switch, and then lowered what appeared to be a rooster's head with a needle in its beak

onto the disc which had been going around and around
but was now slowing down. It seemed to me that the
hole had not been punched in the exact center of the
disc. There was a *squawk!* It sort of sounded like
Chauncey Olcott choking the rooster. Miss Boland
leaped to the controls, which, according to the assorted
sounds that followed, she had yet to master.

"Too bad," said Soup.

"What's too bad?"

"Too bad the Victrola didn't come with instructions."

"Too bad it came at all," I said, and Miss Kelly tapped
her foot. But it was not in time to the music or whatever it was. Sure was a sorry noise. Mrs. Olcott, or who-
ever was inside that box, must have had a heck of a
sore throat. Yet slowly but surely, Miss Boland wrestled
with the problem of tempo, and the Irish rendition of
a twilight song filled the room. Soup covered his ears,
I giggled, and Miss Kelly quietly picked up her ruler,
an act which automatically augmented our musical
appreciation.

Music bubbled from the Victrola like cider from a
jug. Miss Kelly moved a step or two nearer to Soup and
to me. (We always sat together on the same bench.)
Mrs. Olcott continued to ramble through the twilight,
causing Miss Boland to close her eyes in reverie. But
then was when Mrs. Olcott got stuck on a word. From
the Victrola came "*click* . . . weary . . . *click* . . . weary
. . . *click* . . . weary . . . *click,*" and once again Miss
Boland's hand yanked a throttle. The wrong one of

course, which slowed the weary down to a dreary.

"It's a crack," explained Miss Boland.

Mrs. Olcott was given a bit more speed and was also sent back for a running start in order to jump the crack. The song went on and on.

"Whenever I hear this song," said Miss Boland, "it always makes me wish I'd been a dancer. Oh, to be Irene Castle!"

Before I could even turn to Soup and ask who in heck is Irene Castle, our nurse was dancing. Some people are born to dance while others are not. Miss Boland was born to crank a car. But I'll say this for Miss Boland: her lack of grace didn't stop her.

Holding the chair as a helpless partner, she twirled around Miss Kelly's desk with all the ease of a dromedary. Biting my lip, I tried not to laugh, and I didn't dare to even look at Soup, or he at me. He was hanging on to the edge of the desk, fighting the pain. I didn't know who Irene Castle was, but it made me wonder if she was one of the sights at a zoo, like a baby hippo. Then it happened.

Miss Boland stepped on the spindle.

In case you never saw a spindle, it's just a little wooden roller that sort of helps to hold up a chair arm and about as long as a pencil. Not very big, but when you step on one with your eyes closed because you're holding up a chair and pretending to be Irene Castle and you weigh close to three hundred, a spindle can really be false footing. It rolled; and as it did so, Miss Boland's giant white shoe rolled with it. What made things worse was the fact that as Miss Boland stepped on the spindle, she had just come about and was headed due west in the direction of the Victrola. As our nurse opened her eyes, fear was etched across her face and she knew genuine panic in one split moment.

Several splits occurred at once.

My sides split with laughing. So did Soup's. As her leg went out from under her, Miss Boland's legs did the split along with a split in her white uniform about the same length as the Nile. Her errant foot, the one still riding the rolling spindle, raced forward to its fate and split one leg of Miss Kelly's desk. Losing her balance along with the chair she held, Miss Boland reached out, clawing the air in search of any object, great or small, that would provide a strut of safety to help bolster her tottering bulk. As luck would have it, she made the mistake of grabbing the Victrola.

Soup whispered one word: "Timber."

Everything fell, creating a noise that could only be described as a baby hippo landing on Chauncey Olcott or Irene Castle. As the dust cleared, it seemed to Soup and me that the Victrola was the undisputed victor. Mrs. Olcott sang faster and faster with a voice that went up a tree quicker than a squirrel.

I'll give credit to Miss Boland. She was no quitter. Battered and bruised, yes; but here was a woman who never knew the meaning of the word *uncle*. Miss Boland was cut out of tough stuff. Less than ten minutes later,

she had us all in pairs of a boy and a girl, ready for our first rehearsal. Names were thrown into a hat, and Soup got to pick Janice Riker. The angels smiled on me that day because the name of Robert Newton Peck was suddenly linked with none other than—as my trembling fingers unfolded the piece of paper—Norma Jean Bissell!

Twice a week for a month, our dancing classes continued. Soup danced with Janice, and it looked like the best of three falls. Boys were supposed to "lead," but with the combination of Riker *vs.* Vinson, it was Janice all the way. She had a hammerlock on Soup's arm that had him wincing with every step. But I didn't care. Norma Jean Bissell was my constant partner, and it was a heavenly experience just to hold her waist in my right hand and her hand in my left. She seemed to enjoy it, too; and while we danced, she hardly ever picked her nose.

Day after day, Miss Kelly stood as straight and as proud as a picture we had on our wall of Queen Mary of England, waving her ruler ever so slightly to keep cadence as well as conduct. Hour upon hour, Miss Boland taught us the steps. Her partner was always the chair. She looked like a spinning planet. Soup said Mars.

Miss Kelly was right, as always. I had to admit that dancing was fun. Miss Boland seemed to enjoy the chair as a partner. And adding to festive frolic was seeing Soup dance with Janice Riker. Not really with her.

Against her would have described it more aptly, as it was one heck of a struggle. Janice was leading, Soup was following. Here was a girl who could beat every boy in the school at anything you can name (including the Injun Kick) and who seemed doggone determined to add dancing to her list of victories. I'd never seen Soup look so sorrowful. If he got out of line (or out of step), Janice would stomp on his toe. Many was the afternoon I watched poor Soup limp home from school. The look in his eye told me he was plotting something, but I didn't know what.

May danced by.

Suddenly the world of Vermont busted out into June. Fields once brown and barren were now green with new life. The tenth of June was finally here, a Friday afternoon that was as salty and sultry as anticipation could induce. There was no school that morning. We all ate our noon meal at home and arrived at the schoolhouse at two o'clock. Mama and Aunt Carrie came with me, dressed in their best. So was I. My hair was even parted.

And then Soup arrived—on *crutches!*

I saw Mrs. Vinson giving Miss Kelly a long explanation, using phrases like "sprain" and "terrible fall" and "the doctor said" and "just have to keep off it." One of Soup's ankles was bandaged. His face wore an evil smile, all the while his mother was saying something about somebody else. Taking a step or two closer, I overheard the next sentence, which was a genuine shocker.

Soup's mother was saying, "Funny, and it happened just after we'd heard the bad news about that poor little Bissell girl."

Allowing a full second to go by for the sake of appearances, I leaped to Miss Kelly's side, my face looking up into hers. Miss Kelly said that Norma Jean Bissell had been struck down with chicken pox.

Miss Boland arrived with her Victrola.

Streamers of pink and yellow and white crepe festooned the tiny schoolhouse lawn, stretching (and often breaking) from tree to tree. Even though it was daytime, Japanese laterns hung from every available twig, swinging in a spring breeze, a candle burning in each. I helped Miss Boland crank the Victrola but only with my hand and arm. My heart refused to crank up. I could only picture that poor little Bissell girl at home and sick in bed.

We helped Miss Kelly serve punch and cookies to all the grownups who'd come to witness the Spring Dance. I sort of looked for Norma Jean's mother, but she hadn't come. Then we carried out and set up all the folding chairs. It sure was hot work.

Soup did nothing to help. Somebody's mother offered him a chair in the front row and an extra chair to put up his leg on. Then they brought him a glass of punch and a whole darn plate of cookies. For a person with a sprain on his ankle, he sure did smile a lot.

Miss Kelly wore her good dress. It was dark blue with lace around the collar and cuffs. She didn't wear a pencil in her hair, for once, and she sort of looked very nice. She thanked everyone for coming and allowed as all her boys and girls were more than helpful in getting ready for the Spring Dance. All the people clapped.

"Places, children," said Miss Kelly, as Miss Boland braced herself at the Victrola. Her right fist held the crank in a threatening manner. I pitied the Victrola or Mrs. Olcott if they dared to act up on this day. Miss Boland threw the throttle, and Chauncey choked out "Just a Song at Twilight." Miss Kelly gave me a direct order.

I danced with Janice Riker.

But the next day was even worse. I came down with the chicken pox. And the day after that I heard that Janice Riker also had it bad. But I was happiest when I heard about still one more case of the chicken pox.

Soup's.

3

Silver Bullet

"Rob!"

Even though I heard Soup yell my name, I was bending over to fix the knot in my sneaker and figured whatever he wanted wasn't so doggone urgent that it couldn't wait.

POW. Something hit me real hard just as I looked up when I heard it coming down the road. I was halfway up Duggan's Hill, and whatever hit me was halfway down and rapidly moving. It was a soapbox racer, sort of a little car that only coasts downhill, driven by Janice Riker. I caught a quick glimpse of her ratty face as she went rattling by.

Janice was not only the toughest and strongest kid in the whole school. Now she was the meanest thing on four wheels.

"Ha, ha, ha," sang Janice, as she went by in a cloud of dust, knocking me into the cinders. Even her voice was vicious enough to hurt, yet not as much as the gravel in my knee. My pants got tore a tiny bit, and my kneecap was all scraped and bloody. It sort of burned as well as hurt.

Soup was crying.

He probably wouldn't have confessed up to it, but I got a good look at his eyes. And then, as he yanked up his overalls, another look at the cut across his shin, partway between his knee and ankle where the front bumper or whatever it was on Janice's soapbox racer had really smacked him. A welt was on his leg. I had a hunch it smarted as much as my knee.

"Darn you, Janice!" I yelled.

She didn't hear, as by now she was going on down Duggan's Hill and was rounding the turn past Mrs. Biscardi's hencoop. All the kids on the way home from school, big as well as little, had to jump off the road or get whacked by Janice and her stupid car. All it was made of was an old wooden crate with some extra boards nailed on, two large tin cans for headlights, and a steering wheel. And four tires, of course. Plus fat old Janice to add all her weight and make it go downhill like sixty.

"Boy, would I like to get even," said Soup.

"So would I."

"Sure wish *we* had a soapbox racer."

"Yeah. Me too."

"How's your knee?" asked Soup.

"Hurts like heck. How's your shinbone?"

"I'll get over it," said Soup. He got up first, offering his hand to help pull me up on my feet. "Right now, I'm so doggone mad at Janice Riker, I could spit bullets."

"Right," I said, "and if I could spit bullets, I sure know who they'd all get spat at."

"Good old Janice." Soup sniffed his nose.

Instead of spitting a bullet, I did spit some dust out of my mouth. Janice could sure leave people with a bad taste. And on top of that, my sore knee and all, my pantleg was sporting a rip that either the eagle eyes of Aunt Carrie or Mama were sure to spot. I'd probably wind up taking the blame myself. I'd tried before to tell my folks about Janice Riker, the time I came home with a black eye. That, too, had been a gift from Janice, to match my puffy lip. To make it all worse, neither my mother nor Aunt Carrie believed it. In fact, I got given even more grief by trying to pin the cause on "that poor little Riker girl."

Little did they know how easily Janice could whip the daylights out of poor little me, poor little Soup, and also out of any boy in town. That gal had a fist the size and weight of a medium cannonball and could wing a rock like Dizzy Dean. She had hair like a Brillo pad, muscles like Tarzan, the grip of a gorilla, and a breath that was ten degrees hotter than the Chicago Fire. When she'd blow in your face, you'd swear she'd ate a toad for lunch. Just for fun, she could twist your thumb until it met your elbow. Other than these minor habits, Janice Riker was one swell kid.

"One sure thing," said Soup.

"What's that?"

"At least tomorrow's Saturday."

"Yeah. What'll we do, Soup?"

"We need a plan. I bet we can figure out a way to get even with Janice Riker."

"Nobody ever gets even with Janice."

"Oh no?"

"Nope," I said. "I already owe her so many kicks, bites, and socks, it would take me the rest of my life to pay her back. For me, getting even with Janice would be a full-time job."

"Same here," said Soup.

"What's our plan going to do?"

"Get even with Janice in one day," said Soup. "One beautiful day."

All the way home, Soup and I exchanged ideas on how to settle the score. I did most of the talking, while Soup just walked along the road. He sure was in deep thought. But if anyone could invent a scheme evil enough to avenge our wrongs and put Janice Riker in her place for once, I knew it would be Luther Wesley Vinson. When it came to deviltry, Soup was a mastermind. It made me chuckle just to think how clever our plan was going to be and how complete would be Janice Riker's destruction.

"Soup?"

"Quiet. I'm inventing."

"If we had some dynamite, we could blow her up," I said.

"Yeah, but we'd probably blow up ourselves and half the town along with us. We can't destroy the whole world just to knock a few tail feathers off Janice."

"No, I don't guess we can," I said. I was thinking how thoughtful a person Soup was, not wanting to do in the whole world. The day he made *that* decision was certainly a narrow escape for our planet.

Right after Soup did chores at his house and I did mine, he came down and had supper with us. We listened to Jack Armstrong on the radio. It was real exciting, except that I was sort of falling asleep after a tough day and my mind would sometimes mix up the program with the commercials. Jack, Billy, and Uncle Jim were cornered in the jungle, surrounded by a horde of screaming savages. It looked like it would soon be curtains for all three. And the drums! Deep in the jungle on all sides, the savage drums kept up a steady beat. Jack, Bill, and Uncle Jim must have had nerves of tungsten. And the odds were overwhelming.

"Three against a thousand," said Jack.

"We'll never see dear old Hudson High again," said Billy.

"Or ever eat another soggy bowlful of Wheaties," said Uncle Jim.

"That's it!" whispered Jack Armstrong.

"What's it?"

"We eat Wheaties. But not those stupid savages. Our bodies are strong and healthy and fortified with riboflavin. Why those dummies who beat tom-toms wouldn't know a vitamin from a Wheaties box top."

"Box tops are a rip off," said Uncle Jim.

"Just tear along the dotted line," said Billy.

"And we'll send you a savage, absolutely free. You can be the first kid in your neighborhood to own your very own cannibal."

Suddenly the drums were beating louder.

Bang! Bang-bang! Bangity-bang-bang! Bang! Bang! I was too sleepy to count, but it sounded as though Billy and Uncle Jim and Jack Armstrong fired their rifles close to a thousand times. Bang!

"It took a thousand shots," said Uncle Jim, "but those savages who attacked us are all dead."

"All three of them," said Billy.

"Yes, boys and girls, it was three against a thousand. And when the gunsmoke cleared that day in the jungle, we agreed that we had never encountered *three* tougher savages."

"Hey," said Soup, "are you asleep?"

"Not me," I said, straining to open my eyelids as far as half-mast. "Why, I can listen to Jack Armstrong all night and never fall asleep even once."

"Sure you can," said Soup.

"Bedtime," my mother announced.

It was dark outside, so I walked Soup to the place that was halfway between his house and mine, which is

what we always did. Not that we were afraid of the
dark, you understand. Just a gesture of true friendship.
Then we said so long, as Soup ran lickety-split for his
house and I ran for home.

Saturday morning found me up, dressed, my break-
fast eaten, and my chores all done. I was just throwing
the last handful of cracked corn to our ducks when I saw
Soup coming down the pasture on a dead run. His feet
made green footsteps on the early gray dew of the short
meadow grass. He was waving his arms and shouting,
but as he was so out of breath from the run, few of his
words were audible. When he finally pulled up short in
our barnyard, he had to plunk himself down on a bale
of hay to let his breath catch up.

"What's up?" I asked him.

Soup was too winded to answer. So he just winked one
eye, and with his fingertip he put two tiny taps on his
temple, as if to say his brain had come up with an
overnight miracle. Soup had a good brain as far as school-
work was concerned. Miss Kelly wrote a big red A on
his report card as often as on mine. The look on his face
said that his creative juices were flowing, and the bounty
spiced with bile.

"I got it," said Soup, out of breath.

"Got what?"

"Rob, do you know where we're going?"

"No, to where?"

"Guess."

"To see Janice?"

"Almost," said Soup. "Let's go."

"Where we going?"

"We," said Soup, "are going to the Dump."

"What for?"

"To find something."

"It's all the way over on the other side of town."

"Right," said Soup, "it's part of my plan."

"The Dump is part of your plan?"

"Yup. Come on, Rob. Let's get moving."

"Okay, I have to tell my mother where we're going. I don't know why she wants to know where I am every minute, but she sort of gets upset when she doesn't know."

"So does mine," said Soup. "Mothers always want to know a lot of stuff. You know, like . . . where ya been, how'd ya get so dirty, where's your other shoe . . . stuff like that."

"Mothers are curious I guess."

"Yeah," said Soup. "I wonder why."

"Maybe they don't have enough to do."

Mama and Aunt Carrie both had plenty to do when I asked them if Soup and I could go to the Dump. Just as Soup predicted, they started asking lots of questions and wasting away our Saturday. Grown-ups must lie awake nights just thinking up stuff to ask. Finally, they said it was okay and even gave us some apples and dough-nuts to eat, but we both had to be home before chore-time.

The Dump was a real neat place to go. It was a clear

morning and everything was beautiful, as the sun was shining down on all that wonderful junk.

"Sure is amazing," said Soup.

"What is?"

"Look at all the great stuff people actually throw away. This tire's almost good as new."

"Except for a few holes," I pointed out. "Well, now we're here at the dumping grounds, what are we looking for?"

"Wheels," said Soup.

"Honest?"

"We gotta find four wheels. And I'd say six just might be a bit better."

"Wheels for what?"

"A *tank*," said Soup. "We are declaring war on Janice Riker, and you can't win a war without a tank."

"We can build it ourselves."

"You betcha," said Soup, his voice swollen with confidence. "If old Janice can hammer a soapbox racer together, dumb as she is, you and I could build the Brooklyn Bridge."

"That's in our geography book," I said.

"Right," said Soup, looking at a pile of old coat-hangers.

"What kind of a tank will we build?"

"A war tank."

"With guns?"

"Nope," said Soup. "We won't need guns."

"How come?"

"Because we're going to use our tank like a torpedo."

"Like from a submarine."

"You got it. Hey! There's a wheel."

Together we sifted through the mess of discarded materials, and we were rewarded, uncovering an old baby carriage. With three wheels.

"It's missing one, Soup."

"That's okay. We'll find more."

"Wow, look at this." I pointed to an enormous white bathtub. "How about this tub for the body of our tank, Soup? We could ride in it, if the wheels go on."

Soup squinted at the bathtub. I could almost see the blueprints of our war tank spread out in his brain. But then he shook his head.

"Wrong shape."

We saw a stack of old window frames, brass curtain rods, a box of old clothes, a bag of oily rags, a million busted chains, piles and piles of rotten lumber, a pair of red galoshes, an old hat, more tires, a wagon wheel, icebox, ironing board, inner tubes, an old pink sofa with the springs popping out, and lots and lots of spare parts for a car. And an old saddle.

"I wish we could take all this stuff home," I said.

"Wouldn't it be swell," said Soup.

"Can we make a tank?"

"Easy," said Soup. "Curtain rods for axles."

Reaching in his pocket, he produced a roll of black sticky-tape. It was what we always used whenever Soup and I wanted to put something together. Nails and screws were okay, if you have time to hammer. But we were too busy to waste time like that. So we used more than our share of black tape.

"Now," said Soup, "all we gotta find is the *body* of the tank."

"Right," I said.

Sifting through the priceless assembly of discarded chattels, we saw nothing that looked like a suitable chassis. Until we finally turned over an old black hunk of tarpaper and *wow!* There it was! All long and shiny, like a great big silver bullet. It must have been six feet long. For a moment or two neither Soup nor I could speak, such was the degree of our enrapt appreciation.

"That's it," said Soup at last.

"A hot water tank."

There wasn't a single farmhouse kitchen in all Vermont that didn't have a big black cookstove. And attached to it, always in the vertical position of a giant silver silo, was a cylindrical tank for hot water.

"Now that," said Soup, "is what I call a tank that looks like a torpedo."

"Just the right shape," I said.

Rapping the old silver tank with a stick, Soup produced the hollow clanks that apparently passed his rigid standards of tank construction.

"Yup," he said, "it's gallonized iron."

"What's gallonized mean?"

"Well," said Soup, "I reckon it means that it holds a lot of gallons."

"Let's get it on wheels."

"Good idea," said Soup, selecting a rod.

We took wheels off a baby carriage, a lawn mower, a bicycle, and a hobby horse. Then we removed the circular seat from a piano stool. Nothing seemed to fit until the wire and black tape were added. All told, we had nine wheels on our tank. Some touched the ground and some sort of floated. Our tank resembled a railroad car. It was Soup who added the final touch, throwing the old saddle on the tank as though our vehicle was an iron steed.

"Silver Bullet," said Soup, as his hand reached out to pat our tank softly, as though it was the Lone Ranger's horse.

"Soup?"

"Yeah."

"How'll we steer this old girl?"

"That," said Soup, "might be a minor problem."

We ate our lunch. I don't know how, because we were both so excited. Silver Bullet was some invention, saddle and all. She sure was a beauty, like nothing you'd ever seen before. We just sat on a pile of old clothes as we ate, looking at a tank that was part torpedo, part railroad coach, and part horse, held together with wire and tape.

"Come on," said Soup, gulping down the last of his apple and throwing away the core, "let's attack Janice."

"Never thought the day would come," I said, as we headed toward town, pushing Silver Bullet ahead of us, "I'd ever be looking for Janice Riker."

"Me neither."

There wasn't a kid in town who didn't know where Janice's house was. It was a marked spot, like a leper colony. We were up on a hill; behind us, some bushes from where we could look down on the Riker homestead, which was only three houses away from the Baptist Church.

"Hot spit!" said Soup.

Quickly I looked where Soup was pointing. Janice was nowhere in sight, but parked in front of her house was her soapbox racer.

"What'll we do, Soup?"

"Smash it. No sense building a war tank unless you have a good old battle to go along with it."

We stood at the top of Tiller's pasture, looking down a cow path. What a track! All it took was a push here and a tug there to get Silver Bullet pointed down the meadow so that she would hit Janice's car amidships and reduce it to a pile of rubble and poetic justice. Boy, were we clever. I could hardly wait to see Janice Riker's face as Silver Bullet smashed into her soapbox racer. Hers was wood, but *ours* was iron. Gallonized iron!

"Okay," said Soup, "get in the saddle."

"Sure," I said. "You ride behind me."

For a second, for one marrow-chilling moment, I thought Soup was going to suggest that I ride Silver Bullet alone down that hill. But no. He swung his leg up and the two of us occupied the saddle. Slowly at first, we started forward. It seemed sort of high up, but

I guess Soup knew what we were doing.

"Don't forget to lean," he said. We hitched our bodies a bit, and Silver Bullet started her descent.

Faster, faster, faster rolled Silver Bullet, exactly as the deadly torpedo it was meant to be, heading straight for Janice's racer. My hands gripped the horn of the saddle, hanging on for dear life, while Soup's arms were around my waist. Silver Bullet gained speed with every split second. I wanted to close my eyes, but I was too scared. We'd gotten several different sizes of wheels on the darn thing, which made Silver Bullet move less like a torpedo and more like a drunk camel. We weren't on a road. Our trajectory was a cow path down Tiller's pasture that ended up across the road from Janice's house. The ground flew under us.

As I looked down, a wheel came off!

"Lean!" yelled Soup.

We leaned.

But suddenly, so did Silver Bullet. She leaned off to the left so far that she was now way off target. You know, it's a funny thing. But up until now I'd never really pondered much about the fact that Janice Riker lived next door to Mrs. Stetson. The thought never crossed my mind. But now, as Silver Bullet and Soup and I increased our speed, all I could see ahead of us was Mrs. Stetson's vegetable garden, growing bigger and bigger with every bump. My eyes were watering from the speed.

To tell you the honest truth, had Silver Bullet been

actually *shot* from the Lone Ranger's six shooter, she couldn't have gone any faster. I knew that someday Soup and I would have to die, but I never realized until this very moment, that it would be among Mrs. Stetson's tomato plants. Another wheel came off, and then another. But we were shooting across the road too fast to care.

Janice was yelling.

From the corner of my eye, I saw Janice Riker run toward her car, but we were in no danger of hitting her soapbox racer. All I saw now was flowers, Mrs. Stetson's carefully cultivated marigolds, which we plowed through. Then we mowed down primroses, snapdragons, and day lilies, followed by beds of cosmos and shasta daisies, through a bush of peonies, and into the tomatoes, beans, peas, cabbages, and finally between two rows of tall corn. Falling off, Soup and I skidded to a muddy stop between two hills of potatoes. As I sort of hurt all over from the stun of our sudden stop, I couldn't move much. All I heard was Janice Riker's voice laughing at our crash, but then I heard Mrs. Stetson's voice, and she sure wasn't laughing. Peeking through a potato plant, I saw Mrs. Stetson hit Janice Riker with a broom. Janice was trying to point at us, but as Silver Bullet was totally hidden between the rows of corn, all Mrs. Stetson saw was her torn-up garden and Janice's racer, which was all the evidence she needed.

Being in school with old Janice was sure bad enough, but as far as Mrs. Stetson was concerned, having Janice

for a nextdoor neighbor was no picnic either. The destruction of her garden was the last straw. The straws of Mrs. Stetson's big broom landed on Janice and really gave her a smarting. And then Mrs. Stetson attacked Janice's car, and I heard the wood splinter. As it says in the Bible, it sure was a joyful noise.

I always wondered what Mrs. Stetson said (or thought, or did) when she finally found Silver Bullet, saddle and all, between her rows of corn. Soup and I were not around that long to find out.

Maybe she blamed it on the Lone Ranger.

4

Quarter for a Haircut

"Let me see it," said Soup.

"You just saw it."

"But I just want to see it again."

"Okay," I said.

As we walked along the dusty dirt road toward town, I took the coin from my pocket and out into the Vermont air so Soup could take another squint at it. The afternoon sun turned it shiny.

"Gee," said Soup, "a whole quarter."

"And it's all mine," I said.

"Won't be for long."

"I know. I got to turn over the whole doggone thing to the barber, Mr. Petty."

"You can't ask him to cut your hair for free," said Soup.

"Reckon I can't."

"Ya know something, Rob?"

"What."

"If I was a barber, and you came to my barbershop, I'*d* cut your hair for free."

"You really would?"

"Sure would," said Soup, as he kicked a stone and sent it skittering into the milkweed along the roadside. The way he did it, I could tell he was in deep thought.

"Then I sure wish you were Mr. Petty."

"Wishing won't help."

"I know it won't. It's just that I really can't warm to the notion of giving up the quarter."

"If it was *my* quarter," said Soup, "I wouldn't give it to old Petty."

"Well, don't think I cotton to the idea. If I could wangle a haircut for *free*, I'd go get it."

"You would?" Soup asked.

"I sure would."

"Rob . . . today might be your lucky day."

"Today?"

"Yup. Maybe you won't *have* to give your quarter to the barber."

"Oh yes, I do, Soup. My mother said I was to go straight downroad to town and not stop until I got to Mr. Petty's. She didn't seem to care what else I came home with, as long as I left some hair in town."

"Your hair looks okay to me," said Soup.

"When I took a look-see in Aunt Carrie's mirror, it looked okay to me, too. Like it always does."

"Well, it's kind of long in back."

"So's yours," I said.

Soup said, "Always is by the end of August. Seeing as school starts up again next week, I got a hunch *my* mother will pack me off to Mr. Petty's as soon as her nose gets a smell of *your* haircut."

"Probably will," I said.

"Tomorrow she'll hand *me* a quarter and point me toward town."

"And your quarter'll get spent as fast as mine."

"Twenty-five pennies," said Soup. "That would trade for a mighty mess of bubble gum."

"Yeah," I said, "it sure would."

"We could buy enough pink Awful to last us all winter."

I looked at the quarter in my hand. But my mind could suddenly see it in Mr. Petty's hand, all shiny and bright and gone forever, deep into the hidden chambers of his gold cash register where I'd never get it again. And knowing Mr. Petty's true Vermont nature, no one else would get it either.

"It's an honest shame," said Soup, as we were nearing town.

"What is?"

"Giving up a whole winter's worth of Pink Awful to Mr. Petty. I bet his false teeth couldn't even make a dent in it."

"You're telling me," I said. "And if there was any way around it . . ."

Soup stopped with a snap of his fingers. "There *is*."

Anytime I ever saw Luther Wesley Vinson with a glint in his eye as he cracked his fingers, I knew it was time for Robert Newton Peck to be on his guard. Now it meant that Soup had plotted a new course for the money that my mother had given me for a haircut. Mr. Petty and I must both beware.

"What do you mean, Soup?" I was curious, and my curiosity about all kinds of stuff was one of Soup's most lethal weapons in his vast arsenal of deviltry.

"Rob."

"Yeah?"

"Know what I might be when I grow up?"

"No, what?" For a fleeting moment, I thought Soup was changing the subject.

"A barber," said Soup.

Turning the corner into town, we were standing on Main Street. Only a few doors away was an establishment that bore a clearly lettered sign which read: PETTY'S BARBERSHOP. It was the only one in town. It was almost as if Soup could read my thoughts.

"There's the candy store," he nodded in its direction.

"I gotta get a haircut," I said.

"Wouldn't hurt to just look in the window, would it?"

"I don't guess it would," I said, knowing full well that this was a trap, and wanting to step into it with both feet.

As I looked in the window at all the sugar-packed confections that have rotted small teeth by the trillions and delighted dentists to no end, Soup looked across the street at Mr. Petty's.

"Yes," he said, "someday I'll be a growed man and have my own barbershop."

"Honest?"

"Honest. Already gave my cousin a haircut."

"You did, Soup?"

"For *free*."

That was the magic word—*free*. It rang like a little silver bell in a long and lonely night, a beacon in my darkened world. Many was the time Soup and I had poured through mail-order catalogs in quest of *free* offers. Or a *free* sample. It was the fervent devotion to grabbing something for nothing that could hum the heart of every sucker.

"Free," repeated Soup.

He whispered it like an Amen at the end of a long prayer, a stone tablet with one word on it from the God of Israel that could really clinch a deal.

"Could you cut *mine* for free?" I said.

Why I asked such a dumb question would never be discovered, but there was no sense in being too eager to make a decision. Soup walked around me for a turn or two, looking my hair over as if he was buying a horse and giving his own mouth a twist to help his brain do its work. Finally he nodded, indicating that the task of lopping off a curl here and there would not strain his tonsorial talents.

"You know," he said, "I actual could."

"Quick," I said, "let's borrow some scissors."

"Let's get the gum first," said Soup.

Tumbling over each other in our excitement, we took a full second to enter the candy store and confront its ancient proprietor, Mr. Jubert. He was as old as mischief, with a posture bent like a horseshoe from years of stooping to fetch up some penny's worth of inedible and rubbery delight that would result in dental devastation.

"What do *you* want?" asked Mr. Jubert, his old voice creaking with mistrust. Soup and I had been in his store on many an earlier shopping spree, which prompted its proprietor's failing eyesight to make up in vigilance for what it lacked in clarity. Mr. Jubert was wall-eyed. One aging eye looked right at me, sort of, but the other seemed to wander off in search of more interesting images. On this day, however, his other eye followed Soup as a hunter would track a wounded bear. Both his eyeballs gleamed with total and absolute apprehension.

"Bubble gum," said Soup with little hesitation.

"What kind?" Mr. Jubert never made a move, but yet his body seemed cocked as if ready for us to make ours.

"Pink Awful," said Soup, pointing to a tray of goodies.

"How much?" asked old Jubert.

"A quarter's worth," said Soup.

Mr. Jubert had not expected an imposing purchase of such dimension.

"Lemme see it," said Mr. Jubert.

"See what?" I said.

"The quarter," he croaked.

My hand shook a bit as I exposed my total worth to Mr. Jubert. The expression on his face did not soften. He peered over the two half-moons of his spectacles to inspect my money. Without a word, the ancient spine assumed its ancient arc . . . down, down, down, sliding open the glass door at his knee. His dirty fingers reached inside. Without looking, without counting, his hand clutched exactly twenty-five rectangles. The old backbone unbent and lifted him up, up, up; until the two-dozen-plus-one sprawled before us on the cloudy counter. Soup and I both reached for the trove of dusty packages.

"Not so fast," said Mr. Jubert.

Before I could say even a word, Mr. Jubert's other hand struck like a cobra and closed on my quarter, snatching it from my fingers. I didn't even see it disappear. It just went.

The gum was now mine.

Yet somehow I couldn't bring myself to touch it. Neither could Soup. We just stood and stared at the twenty-five pink packages. The brand was Pink Awe. But nobody called it that. Some wit had thought of calling it Pink Awful, as it was pink; and to the prejudiced palate of anyone except a kid, tasted awful. Perhaps as the creator had bestowed the nickname, he was in the process of trying to pry a pink wad from the sole of his shoe. The name stuck as well.

"Anything else?"

"No, thank you." I answered Mr. Jubert's question.

"Do you have a pair of shears, Mr. Jubert?" Soup asked.

"*Shears?* What for?" Mr. Jubert scowled.

"I want to cut something," was Soup's resourceful reply.

Normally, it would be my guess that Mr. Jubert was not a willing lender (chattels being as closely guarded as his emotions). He looked at Soup with a suspicious eye, as his other eye sighted on me.

"What you aim to cut?"

"A lock of my hair." I said. "We need it for a reason."

"It's for Sunday School," said Soup. "The lesson is on Samson."

Mr. Jubert, wondering if he should support such a worthy cause as religious education, studied the pair of us for a full moment before placing the shears on the counter beside the pile of Pink Awful. Those shears were the biggest shears in the whole world, I was thinking, and probably could trim a tree. Soup picked them up, holding them in both hands as they appeared to have too much heft for just his right. He brought the shears close to the back of my neck, making a few practice snips (cutting nothing) the way Mr. Petty usually does.

"Go do it outside," said Mr. Jubert.

We hurriedly exited.

As we left, I took note that Mr. Jubert allowed as how he would keep our gum until we returned with his tool. To call those gigantic shears anything that resembled barbering scissors would have been a profanity. They were sure big.

Once outside, it was amazing how fast Soup cut my hair. Any wisp or curl that stuck out into the Vermont weather got whacked off. Those big shears made one heck of a metallic noise with the bang of their blades. *Clank.* Rang out like a church bell. Down at my feet another ring (of curls) surrounded my blue sneakers.

"Hey, Soup?"

"Yeah." *Clank. Clank.*

"Don't take off too much. Winter's coming."

"It's still August and hot as a hayloft. Oops, I just made a mistake. You gotta hold still." *Clank Clank Clank.*

"What kind of mistake?"

"Well, I sort of went too deep in one spot. Maybe I can sort of even it off." *Clank.*

"How?"

"Just cut a bit here . . ." *Clank* "and over there . . ." *Clank* "so's it don't show up as bad."

"What don't show?"

"Your skin."

"You mean my *scalp??*"

"Yeah." *Clank Clank.* "Oops!"

"What happened?"

"Just another mistake." *Clank Clank Clank.*

"Don't you think you took enough off?"

"Hold still. I'm not taking any more off." *Clank.*

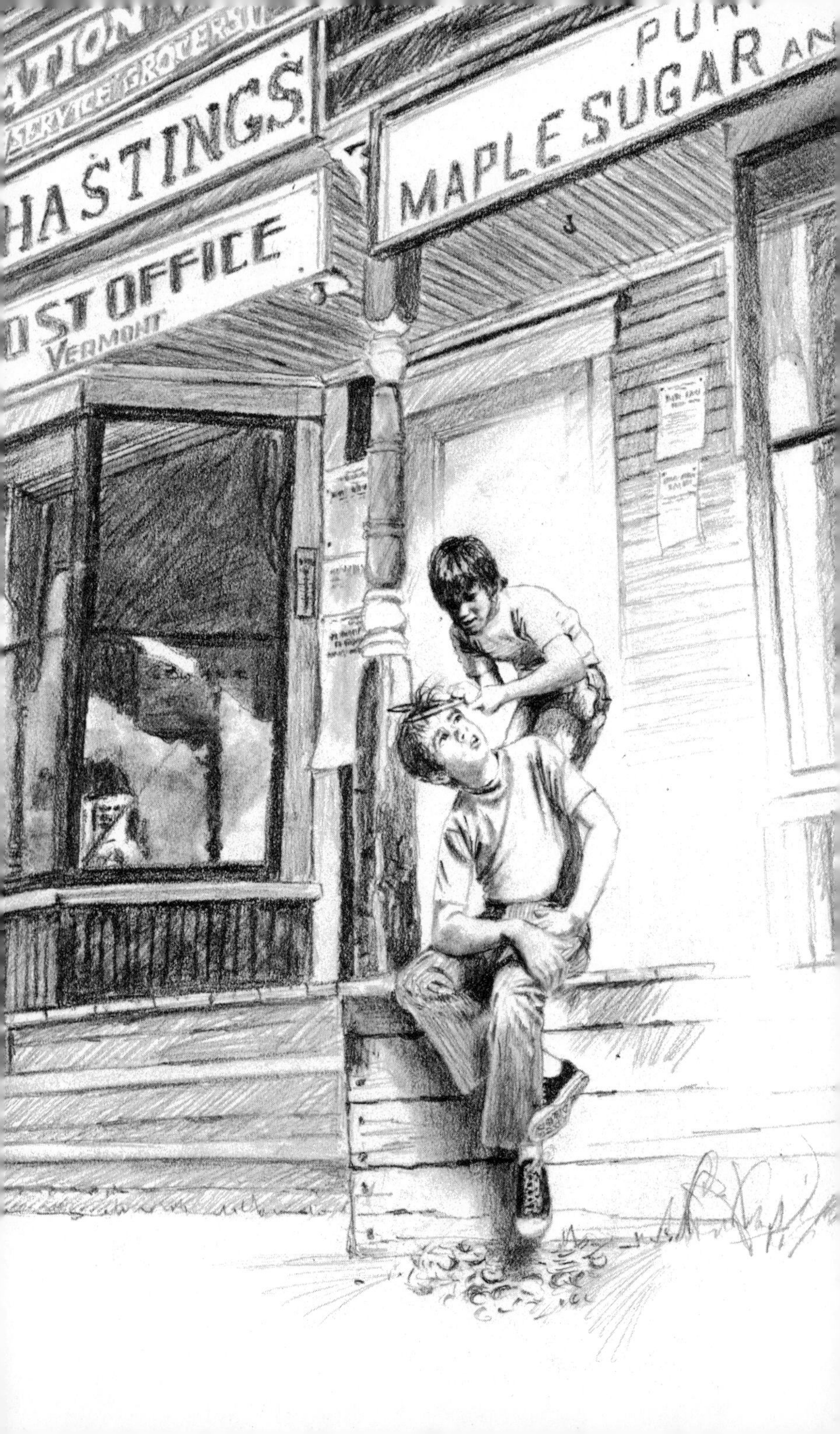
SERVICE GROCERS
HASTINGS
OST OFFICE
VERMONT
MAPLE SUGAR

"You're still cutting."

"Not really cutting. Just kind of evening it."

"Do a good job, Soup."

"Don't worry."

I wasn't one to worry much. Except when Soup assured me that I didn't have a worry in the world. Only then did my hands start to sweat, and I looked at my palms. They were wet. *Clank Clank Clank.*

"Oops," said Soup.

"Another mistake?"

"Sort of. But it's small. No one will ever notice 'cause it's right next to one of the big."

"One of the big *what?*"

"Big mistakes." *Clank.* "There, I'm all done."

"You sure put a lot of hair down my neck. How do I look?"

Without waiting to hear Soup's reply, I turned to find my reflection in the candy store window. I sure did look different. No denying I'd had a haircut. It didn't look real bad. Then again, you wouldn't say it looked real good, either. Twisting away from the glass, I saw Soup down on his knees. Using his hands, he swept up my cut-off hair and then stood up, stuffing my hair into his pocket.

"Let's go," said Soup.

Returning the shears to the counter of the candy store, we started to pick up the gum. Old Jubert had his back to us as we walked in. Turning, he saw us. Then he saw *me!* His head bobbed forward like a turkey and his mouth popped open. It was the first time I'd ever seen Mr. Jubert's face change its look. He darn near smiled.

Soup and I chewed gum all the way home. We'd chew a sheet of Pink Awful, pop some bubbles with it, and then when all the flavor was gone, we'd spit a pink cud into the dust of the road and help ourselves to fresh. Sure was fun. It was a long hike from town, as both the Pecks and the Vinsons were uproad folk, and by the time our house was sighted, our jaws were as weary as our legs.

"Stop," ordered Soup.

I stopped—chewing and walking.

"Rob," he said, "you're my pal. Right?"

"Yeah, I'm your pal."

"So I can't let your mother and your Aunt Carrie see you the way you are. What's the first thing those two'll do when you get back?"

"They'll inspect my haircut."

Soup nodded. "That's why we got to do a patch job."

"A patch job? Like on a *tire?*"

"Sort of." Soup spat out his gum, this time into his hand. He rubbed it on my head, around and around, sometimes in small circles and then in bigger ones.

"How come you're putting bubble gum in my hair, Soup?"

"So the hair'll stick."

"What hair?"

Soup reached into the pocket of his corduroys and came up with a handful. "*This* hair."

He began to put back hair on the places he'd rubbed on the gum.

"Suppose it comes off," I said.

"Pink Awful *never* comes off," said Soup.

But not even Soup could be right all the time. At the hands of my mother, the hair and most of the Pink Awful *did* come off when my head was held under the pump. And before I was sent to bed with no supper, my overalls also came off.

And about a week later the awful pink spots from her hairbrush came off my behind.

5

Havoc on Halloween

"Hurry," said Soup.

He was standing first on one leg and then on the other, with his hand on the inside knob of our kitchen door. Aunt Carrie was sitting at the kitchen table, drinking a cup of tea, watching Soup turn the knob back and forth.

"Stand still," my mother commanded. "You want to be a ghost, don't you?"

"Yes," I said.

"Then stop your fidgeting until I pin up your sheet, or else you'll drag it all the way to the church." My mother's voice sounded strange as her mouth was full of pins.

"I'm a pirate," said Soup.

Mama pricked me with a pin, and I jumped and

yelled. Then she let out a long sigh. Maybe it was because it was about the tenth time that Soup said he was a pirate. His left eye was covered with a black patch. His mother had painted a long curly mustache under his nose and wrapped a tube of cardboard around his shin, from ankle to knee, so he'd look like he had a wooden leg. Stuck in the silk scarf around his waist was a long piece of flat wood on which a shorter cross-piece had been attached for a handle by a bent-over nail. Soup said it was a sword.

"I've changed my mind," I said to Mama. "I want to be a pirate, like Soup."

"You're a ghost," said Mama, "and that's all there is to it."

"The holes aren't over my eyes right," I said to Mama, who was on her knees in front of me, snapping in a silver safety pin as fast as she could.

"We'll be late and miss all the games," said Soup.

"I see no reason," said Aunt Carrie, "for the two of them to go *alone* all the way into town. It's way after dark."

"Because," said Mama, "the Halloween party is at the Baptist Church, and I for one think it's nice they were asked. They don't get to go many places. And besides, Bess Tanner will be there to keep an eye out for them and to bring them home."

"If we ever get there," said Soup.

Off into the dark we scampered, running as fast as we could down the dirt road toward town. We ran until we just had to stop for breath and lean against the big elm tree that was at the curve of the road. It sure was dark.

"Come on, Rob."

"Here we go," I said.

"Look at me," said Soup. "I can run just like a pirate." He galloped along in a pronounced limp.

"This is how a ghost runs," I said, flapping my arms to wake the corners of my white sheet, moaning as I ran. Finally we slowed down to a trudge.

"Yo, ho, ho, and a bottle of rum," said Soup.

"Huh?"

"That's what pirates say."

"Who said?"

"I asked Miss Kelly. Because I told her we were going to the Halloween party at the Baptist Church. Then you know what she said?"

"What'd she say?"

"Miss Kelly said that while I was at the Baptist Church, best I kept to saying yo, ho, ho and a bottle of pop."

"*Rum* sounds better," I said.

"Maybe to a pirate," said Soup, "but according to Miss Kelly, not to a Baptist."

We nearly made it. Finally we got to the top of Sutter's Hill, out of breath from running, so we straddled the fence for a while to let our wind catch up. The moon had been behind a cloud, but just then that old October moon came out of hiding. It just sort of hung in the sky like a yellow cookie, sugary enough to eat. Sud-

denly, even the crops were all creamy with moonlight.
And that was when we saw it; there it was, before our
very eyes . . . Mr. Sutter's patch of pumpkins.

"Let's go see 'em," said Soup.

"He'll sick the dogs on us."

"No he won't."

Jumping down off the fence, the pirate and the ghost
ran through the field of pumpkins. They were full-grown
and really ripe for harvest. Soup stopped in his tracks,
lifting up his black patch as if he didn't believe his other
eye. I looked where he pointed, and sure enough, there
was the biggest old pumpkin in the whole State of Vermont. I wanted to say something, but the words that
came to mind just weren't big enough or orange enough
to fit the size.

"That's some vegetable," said Soup.

"You know, Soup . . . if God were to carve a jack-o-
lantern, that there is the one pumpkin He'd pick."

"Let's pick it," said Soup.

"And do what with it?"

"Take it to the party."

"No dice," I said.

"How come?" asked Soup.

"Well, I can't forget so soon what my mother said
about behaving ourselves or we wouldn't ever be invited
next year or ever again."

"You're *supposed* to pick a pumpkin at Halloween."

"Not one of Mr. Sutter's pumpkins."

"What's so special about these?" said Soup.

"Rolly said old Sutter's got himself a shotgun loaded up with rocksalt that can shoot a mile."

"Shotguns don't shoot a mile."

"His does."

"Who said?"

"Rolly McGraw. He said when he stole apples last fall, old Sutter gave him both barrels. He said his butt burned for a week."

"Maybe you're right, Rob. But wouldn't it be great to walk into that party with a pumpkin this big."

"Real great. But we dasn't."

"Know who's going to be there?" said Soup.

"Who?"

"Norma Jean Bissell."

Soup sure could say magic words to turn one object into another. Words that suddenly, presto-change-o, turned a ghost into a pumpkin thief.

Soup sat on the big pumpkin and just sort of whistled to himself, like he didn't care whether or not we picked the pumpkin and toted it to the party.

"Let's see if we can lift it," I said.

With me on one side and Soup on the yonder side, we picked it up. It was heavy as heck. Yet we started toward the fence with it, heading back to the dirt road. But suddenly we reached the end of our vine. As the big pumpkin tore out of our hands, it hit the soft brown earth with a *thud*.

"Got a knife, Rob?"

"I had one, but Aunt Carrie's got it now."

"How come she's got it?"

"All I did was cut the clothes line."

"Is that all?"

"Yeah, but her underwear was on it."

"Find a sharp stone," said Soup.

To find a bit of rock in the topsoil of Vermont is simple. Locating an edge to chop through a pumpkin vine as thick as a rope takes longer. But we did it. Tug upon tug, we somehow hefted the pumpkin up and over the fence. We carried it another fifty feet to the top of Sutter's Hill, but it seemed like we'd carted a camel across the Sahara.

"Let's set it down, Soup."

"Fine with me."

We did.

"I can't pack that thing another step."

"Neither can I," said Soup.

Below in the town, we could see the lights of the Baptist Church aglow with festivity. People were singing. And then there'd be a burst of laughter.

"The party's started," said Soup.

"We'll never make it." I kicked the pumpkin.

"Never say die, Rob, old sport. All we need now is something to carry it in."

"Yeah, like a yoke of oxen and a stone boat."

"Nah," said Soup. "There's gotta be a way."

"Maybe we best just go to the party without it."

"Could," said Soup, "but it'd be a dirty shame to give up on the job now that we got it this far."

"*This* far? We barely got it cross fence. The Baptist Church is all the way down the hill. If we roll it down, it'll smash to bits."

"Roll. That's what'll make it easy," said Soup.

"Easy?"

"Yeah. All we need now is a *wheelbarrow*."

Leaving the pumpkin in the ditch beside the road, covered with some leafy twigs off a red maple, we ran down the hill into town. We couldn't find a wheelbarrow. A contraption like that is always simple enough to stumble across when you're not in search of one. But when you wander around in the dark, with no flashlight, dressed in a sheet long enough to trip on and with the eye holes usually in the wrong place, finding a wheelbarrow is no snap. We looked and we looked.

Miss Kelly always said that just when you think it's time to give up, that's the time to try harder. She was referring to a particular problem I had that seemed to be hopelessly embedded into the mystery of multiplication. But I suppose her lesson would apply to beating the bushes for a dumb old barrow. Then I saw one, behind the woodshed of a dark house.

"Soup!"

"Be quiet."

"I found one."

"Hush, or somebody'll find us. A great pirate *you'd* be."

"I'm not a pirate. I'm a ghost."

"Help me," said Soup. "It's kind of big."

Soup lifted up one handle of the wheelbarrow and I took the other. Not until this moment did I ever realize that a wheelbarrow pushed through the night is the noisiest thing on one wheel. The big barrow sure was heavy. How we even got it halfway up Sutter's hill I'll never know, unless it was pure grit.

"I can't push another inch," I said.

"Yes, you can," said Soup.

"Let's give up the whole stupid idea."

"Okay. But I got a hunch."

"What's your hunch."

"I bet old Norma Jean Bissell never saw a pumpkin big as ours," said Soup.

"You don't mean ours. It's Mr. Sutter's."

"He's got a thousand. He won't care. Come on, let's keep pushing."

Up, up, up Sutter's Hill we went, Soup and me and the wheelbarrow in the lead. Even though I must have trudged up that old grade a million times on the way home from school, I never knew until now that Sutter's Hill was some sort of an Alp that had got misplaced when the earth got formed.

"Just remember," grunted Soup.

"Remember what?"

"How simple it'll be to come back. Why, it'll be easy as pie, as it's all downhill."

"Yeah," I said. "It'll near to float."

We struggled upward, pushing the wheelbarrow ahead of us. It must have outweighed a tractor. Sweat was all over my face, and I wanted to take off my sheet. Trouble is, I'd never put it back on right. Sutter's Hill was a dirt road. Just gravel that was rife with small pebbles, which made your foot slip. You couldn't seem to dig in to get a good solid push. We'd charge for about half a yard and then rest.

"I'm roasting," said the pirate.

"So am I," the ghost agreed.

"Maybe we oughta scrap the whole stupid idea."

"Remember what Miss Kelly said."

"What'd she say?" Soup asked.

"Well, I can't exactly remember how she said it, but it had a lot to do with sticking to a job. And not to give in when the going got tough."

"I wonder," said Soup.

"About what?"

"If *her* going was as tough as *our* going."

Closing my eyes and straining on my one handle of the barrow, I tried to see the face of Norma Jean Bissell as I casually strolled into the party at the Baptist Church, holding that big pumpkin. As I stepped on the edge of my sheet, I heard it rip.

"Soup, my sheet just got tore."

"That's too bad," grunted Soup, without even as much as a wisp of genuine sympathy.

"We're almost up," I said.

"Keep pushing."

"I am. Hard as I can."

"Heave ho," said Soup. "That's what a pirate says."

"How come you know so much about pirates?"

"I just do," said Soup.

"You sure don't know much about wheelbarrows."

"How so?"

"Well, if you ask me, instead of taking the barrow *up* to the pumpkin, we should of took the pumpkin *down* to the wheelbarrow."

"Now you tell me," said Soup.

"Cheer up. We're near to the top."

"We've had some dumb ideas, Rob. But this here is got to be the runt of the litter."

"I can't push much farther. My arms hurt."

"So do mine," said Soup. "They ache like holy heck if you want the straight of it."

"Bet mine hurt worse than yours."

"I bet they don't."

"Sure they do. Because I'm a year younger than you are, Soup."

"But I got more muscle to ache with."

"Maybe so."

"No maybe about it. Push."

"I'm pushing."

We did it. Don't ever ask me how, but we finally rattled that dirty old wheelbarrow clear up to the tippy-top of Sutter's Hill. Like a dream come true. Then we both collapsed on the grass beside the road.

"I'm all played out," said Soup.

"Me too."

"Best we get to the party."

"Yeah, 'cause Mrs. Tanner will be on the lookout for us."

"Come on, Rob."

"Now what?"

"We got to load our pumpkin into the barrow."

"I was afraid you'd say that."

"You want Norma Jean to see it, don't you?"

"Yes," I said. "But it's starting to mean less and less."

"Look, Rob . . . we gotta take the barrow back. Which means we might as well take the pumpkin down with it. Right?"

"Right."

"So let's go," said Soup.

"Okay."

We rolled the pumpkin as tenderly as we could, and heavy though it was, we managed to hoist it up and into the bin.

"Now to turn the doggone thing around," said Soup.

Coming about, we finally had ourselves and the loaded barrow pointed downhill, right toward the Baptist Church.

"Ready?" I said.

"Ready as we'll ever be," said Soup.

"Here goes."

"This'll be the easy part. All downhill."

"Good old gravity," I said.

Holding it like I would a baseball bat, my fingers took a purchase on my handle, as Soup grabbed his. It was sure heavy. We had to really strain to move it all along the level. Forward we went. I saw the prow of the barrow drop down, and we were on the hill. The wheelbarrow moved easier and easier. Soup was right. From now on, it was downhill all the way. The wheelbarrow rolled right along, almost as if it knew that its destination was the front door of the Baptist Church.

"Easy as pie," said Soup.

"Pumpkin pie." I giggled and so did Soup.

"With whip cream on it."

"And ginger."

The wheelbarrow picked up speed, so quickly that it sort of kicked up like a whipped horse. I thought the handle was going to rip right out of my fingers.

"Hang on," I said.

"If I can," said Soup.

We were running now, full speed, smack down Sutter's Hill and heading full tilt toward the party. Ahead of us, the giant pumpkin bounced around inside the bin of the barrow. I felt like we'd stolen the moon.

"We're out of control!" yelled Soup.

"Turn it. Do anything, anything!"

"Can't."

The front door of the Baptist Church grew bigger and bigger, rushing toward us like a mad monster. My feet hardly touched the ground. I was too frightened to hang on much longer, yet frightened even more to let loose. Soup was screaming and so was I.

"Stop," wailed Soup.

From the street, there was one step up to the door

of the Baptist Church. The door was closed. Actually it was a double door, painted red, coming at us like a giant red square. I tried to let go of the handle of the wheelbarrow, but my cramped fingers would not unlace. Just then the one front wheel of the barrow hit the one step, and several things happened in rapid succession. The wheelbarrow, which had a split second earlier been traveling down Sutter's Hill at a hundred miles an hour, stopped with a buck. The pumpkin flew out and straight ahead. Soup and I tripped over the suddenly immobile bin of the barrow. The big pumpkin smashed open both the doors of the Baptist Church, rolling at full steam down the center aisle. The aisle was waxed wood, causing Soup and me to slide on our bellies right behind the pumpkin. Pew after pew flew by.

Events did not stop there.

I didn't see Norma Jean Bissell. But as I hurtled forward toward all the surprised faces, I *did* see Mrs. Stetson. She let out a very loud scream, as though the Devil himself had joined the Baptist Church. Ahead of us, kids were bobbing for apples in a huge tub of water. An adult was among them. Raising his dripping face from the tub of water, with an apple in his mouth, was none other than Mr. Hiram Sutter. The apple fell from his teeth, but his mouth remained wide open in the shock of seeing things racing right at him.

Pins were sticking into me from all angles.

Hitting the little step in front of the altar, the pumpkin leaped high. For a second, it hung in the air like a huge orange planet and then landed into the giant tub of water with a sounding splash. Mr. Sutter was drenched to the skin. Just as the tub toppled over, Soup slid into Mrs. Stetson. As I slid into Mr. Sutter, I heard Mrs. Tanner bust out laughing.

Water, water everywhere.

Sometimes, they say, when a person has a temper tantrum, cold water helps to cool off the disposition. Yet all that wet didn't do too much for Mr. Sutter. Even less for Mrs. Stetson who screamed like an alley cat.

"Luther Vinson!" I heard her holler at Soup.

One of the eye holes in my sheet was over my nose, and the other had sort of wandered off somewhere near my chin, so I didn't see what was going on. But the tone of the voices seemed to get the idea across that nobody was overly happy at the sudden turn of events, including our arrival.

"Where'd ya git that pumpkin?" said a deep and humorless voice that sounded like a very wet Mr. Sutter.

"We found it," said Soup.

"Yeah," said Mr. Sutter, "and I know where."

Pulling a hole around to be over my left eye, half my vision was restored just in time to see Mr. Sutter grab Soup and shake the living daylights out of him. I thought of crying, but it probably wouldn't have saved me; nobody could see my tears as my head was under the sheet. Not for long. I was quickly unveiled by the irate arm of Mrs. Stetson, who, as she did so, stuck her hand with one of my pins. She was very wet and very angry.

"Robert Peck!" she yelped. Her face was near to purple.

"We were invited," I said.

It didn't do any good. Mrs. Stetson yelled "Robert Peck" at the top range of her voice. Somebody, who felt a lot like Mr. Sutter, took hold of me and I shook like a malted. Then Soup and I were sent to the back closet to fetch mops and a bucket, and after the two of us sopped up the water, we were assigned other duties. The pumpkin was reloaded into the wheelbarrow, by us, and taken back to where we'd cut it from its vine. All the way up Sutter's Hill. It was amazing how strong we became with Mr. Sutter behind us with a switch in his hand. Then we brought the wheelbarrow back to where we'd borrowed it and headed back to the church.

I never even saw Norma Jean Bissell, but both Soup and I sure saw enough of Mr. Sutter and Mrs. Stetson. Other kids got to play. We missed all the games. It was one heck of a long evening. By the time Mrs. Tanner dropped me off at home, both Soup and I were sound asleep. Talking woke us up. We held our breaths when we heard the topic of conduct.

"Were they angels?" my mother asked.

"No," said Mrs. Tanner, shooting a wink in my direction, "they were a pirate and a ghost."

6

Turkey Trot

"Listen," said Soup.

As both Soup and I stopped dead in our tracks, we strained our ears. Sure enough, we heard it, coming from a long ways off. We were walking downhill through Wicker's Woods, due east, when Soup first heard the noise, which was really strange. Sort of spooky.

"What is it?" I said.

"Beats me," said Soup. "Sounds sort of like a big crowd of people all talking at once." He wiped his nose on the edge of his mitten.

"Yeah, it does in a way."

"Let's go see, Rob."

"Okay."

We raced through the crisp November woods, kicking brown leaves into the air with a dry rustle that crackled with its own happiness. As we scampered through the autumn forest, the sound that we earlier had heard was now smothered.

We stopped.

"Hear it?" said a breathless Soup.

"Now it's louder."

"We must be getting closer. Let's go."

Again we ran, until Wicker's Woods ended in a rail fence. Soup vaulted over and I was fast on his heels. We were in an open field. We'd never been this far before on any of our Saturday morning hikes. Our feet jumped across row after row of corn stubble. You could tell by the size of the stumps that it hadn't been sweet corn. It had been field corn, for silage. Now that we were in the open instead of traveling through fallen leaves, I could hear the noise even as we ran. My feet wanted to call a halt; but as Luther Vinson raced ahead of me, I swore to myself that somehow Robert Peck would keep up. Someday, I told my own thoughts, I would really beat Soup at something. But it might not be today, and it sure wouldn't be at running across this old corn field, as Soup's legs were an inch longer than mine.

It was getting really loud.

The strange noise seemed to move toward us as we ran. Soup finally pulled up short and so did I. There we were, atop a hillside, trees to the left of us and some houses to the right. Below, straight ahead, was a fenced-in area that must have held at least a thousand turkeys.

What a racket they made.

"Here 'em gobble?" said Soup.

"I can even *smell 'em* gobble."

Everywhere we looked, there was a big old turkey walking around and pecking at the brown earth. The turkeys were white, turning the great yard into a blizzard, as each snowflake strutted to and fro among all the others, like they were all knowingly braiding some giant white quilt for winter.

"Turkeys," said Soup.

"How many do you think there are?"

"Shhh!! I'm counting," said Soup.

I giggled. "Don't forget to count Tom."

"Count who?"

"Tom," I said. "All turkeys are called Tom, except for the girl turkeys."

"What are *they* called?"

"I used to know but I forgot."

We sat on a log, still short of breath, and panting from our footrace, counting all those countless white birds. Soup liked to cipher with his finger poking the air in front of his face, while I sat on that hard old log and tried to think of the name for female turkeys.

"There's too many to add up," said Soup. "I lost count."

"And I can't remember what you call a turkey that's a girl."

"Who cares about dumb old *girls*," said Soup.

"Girls aren't dumb."

"Yes they are."

"Some are," I said. "But not Norma Jean Bissell."

"Is she sweet on you?" asked Soup, wrinkling his nose up as he always did when he talked about taking a laxative or about girls. "Well, *is* she sweet on you or isn't she?"

"Sort of."

"Then she's dumb," said Soup. "And you're dumb to be sweet on Norma Jean Bissell."

"No I'm not. I don't even like her."

"Heck you don't."

"Well, maybe a bit. Doggone it, Soup, lay off . . . so's I can recollect the name of a girl turkey."

"Tom?"

"No! It's a girl's name," I said.

"Ted? Or maybe Tim."

Soup got me to giggling, and all of a sudden I knew we'd discovered another game to have at.

"Trudy?" I said.

"Thelma," said Soup.

"Toby."

"That's a funny name for a girl," said Soup. "I know what Janice Riker's parents should've named Janice."

"What?" I said.

"Tank."

I almost fell off the log, laughing so hard. "Either that or Tarantula."

"Instead of her," said Soup, "I'd rather get bit by a spider. Say! Wouldn't it be something to watch a black widow bite old Janice?"

"Yeah," I said. "And then to see that poor old spider curl up and die." We both chuckled forever over that. I was holding my sides, they hurt so much. Tears were filling my eyes. Soup wiped his, and said "Stop" a couple of times in a weak voice. My stomach was starting to hurt.

"Hey," said Soup in a soft voice.

"Hey what?"

He pointed behind us and to the left where the pines were thick. I looked hard, but couldn't see a doggone thing.

"Something's moving," said Soup in a whisper.

"Like what?"

"Can't make it out. Wanna go investigate?"

"I'm game."

"I'll be the Lone Ranger," said Soup.

We ran toward the woods, keeping low like the Lone Ranger and Tonto. Soup almost always got to be who he wanted to be. I got to be Tonto a lot. Once into the pines we threw ourselves forward, landing with our bellies snug to a soft brown carpet of pine needles. Nothing was moving.

"You're seeing things, Soup."

"No I'm not. Honest."

Whenever old Soup said "honest," I knew he wasn't just pulling my leg. He was serious. The tone of his voice said that he was giving me the straight of it, and so not to doubt his word.

"Over there," said Soup.

"Where?" I felt my eyes grow bigger.

Soup nodded his head off to the left, pointing an arm into the blacky-green of the pines. As I followed his glance, I saw a gray object duck behind a tree trunk. Soup wasn't kidding. He really did spot something strange.

"I know what it is," said Soup.

"So do I."

"What?"

Soup had me trapped. I really didn't know what we saw, except that it was gray, sort of. And pretty big. It couldn't be a ghost, because ghosts were just a lot of make believe. Just pretend.

"Come on, Rob."

Soup ran, and I ran, too, as fast as we could. So fast we were darn near flying. My eye caught a flash of gray, and then another.

Gobble!

It was a turkey. A big white turkey, and my guess said it was bigger and heavier and stronger than all the other turkeys we just got through looking at back yonder. Must have been a banished king.

"A turkey," I said, as if Soup didn't know.

"No kidding," said Soup in a half-smile, with just one corner of his mouth and not the other.

"Maybe we can catch him," I said.

"Him? Maybe it's a *her*."

"So then we'll catch *her*."

"Or it," said Soup.

Until today, I was thinking as we chased that bird, I never knew that a turkey could run so speedy. It didn't fly. But it sure did cover the ground, in and out of the pines, heading toward the County Road. Sometimes we were fast enough to keep that old turkey in sight, and sometimes not. Once or twice we thought he'd got away. But then we spied him again and gave chase. I was puffing.

"I'm pooped," said Soup. He leaned against the trunk of a sassafras in order to wait for his wind. Another tree was handy, so I hugged it to hold me up.

"I see him," I said.

"Who cares?" said Soup.

"Aren't we going to catch him?"

"Not according to him," said Soup. "I don't guess that old turk wants to be caught."

"You give up awful easy," I said.

"Look," said Soup, "it ain't that we give up easy. That there turkey just gives up awful hard."

"We can corner him."

"Fine," said Soup, "if we had a corner."

"Come on," I said.

"There he goes!" Soup pointed.

There was suddenly a small stone inside my right shoe, but not big enough of a tribulation to stop for. Not when that old turk was so much in our vicinity. It would sure be a crying shame to wash out now, just when we were gaining on that bird.

Ahead was a culvert.

This I knew, because I'd once been to Ally Tidwell's house (which was nearby) and the two of us had caught a frog at the mouth of one end. The culvert was just a big old tube that went under the County Road like a tunnel, from one ditch to the other. Veering over to the shoulder of the road as I ran, I caught a look at the turkey, who just ducked into one end of the culvert. Soup and I both got the flash of an idea at the same time.

"I'll take this side," I yelled.

Soup said, "And I'll head him off on the other end."

He was trapped!

Jumping clear of the road, I ducked down to look into the culvert and there was that turkey, halfway through the tunnel. A second later I saw the happy face of Luther Vinson. Between us was the turkey, looking first at me and then at Soup. He knew he was in a pickle. Back when Ally Tidwell and I caught the frog, it was May or early-on June, and there had been a few inches of water flowing under the dirt road from one side to the opposite. But now it was November, the water was gone. The culvert was bone dry from one end all the way through to the other.

"We got him," said Soup. His voice came through the culvert real funny, sort of like he was down in the bottom of a well. I could see him as he was at a squat in the circle of light.

"Sure have," I said to Soup.

The turkey ran down toward where Soup was waiting. Soup made a noise and clapped his hands, sending that big white bird back toward me. He sure was big. Darn near filled up the culvert like a cork. He looked to be near big as a pony. Coming close up to me, I was afraid he was fixing to take a peck at my face.

"Yah!" I said. He turned and showed me the big white puff of his rump and his yellow feet. "Soup, when he comes your way, grab him."

"No thanks."

"Whaddaya mean, no thanks?" I said.

"I don't want to. You do it. Or are you scared?" asked Soup.

"Well, not really. I just never took much to turkeys."

"Me neither," said Soup, "and this turkey looks like he don't cotton too much for me."

The old turkey let out a *gobble gobble*, and I've got to admit I jumped, hitting my head a crack on the rim of the culvert. It sure did smart. We continued to talk back and forth in our funny hollow voices that bounced around inside the culvert.

"What'll we do?" I said.

"One of us," said Soup, "will have to volunteer."

"What's *volunteer* mean? Is it like a fireman?"

"Sort of. It's when you volunteer for a dangerous mission, like the Green Hornet."

"Oh," I said.

"Rob?"

"Yeah."

"Do you want to volunteer?"

"Not a whole lot. You?"

"Nope," said Soup. "But I just got another idea."

"Yeah? Like what?"

"We'll use strategy."

"Is it something like volunteer?"

"In a way."

"What's your plan?" I said.

"Someone has to crawl into the culvert and grab the turkey."

"You thought of it first."

"So I get to pick the volunteer. My job is to create a diversion."

Only one volunteer on Soup's roster possessed the skill, the courage, not to mention the stupidity, to enter a culvert and have it out with a turkey that was becoming increasingly annoyed, running from Soup to me to Soup to me. There was a look in his eye that promised hostility by the carload, hatred by the hatful, discomfort by the lump. This turkey was not chicken. This bird was as big as a goat. And yet all the volunteer had to do was crawl inside the culvert, crawl right up to the turkey, and grab it. Simple. A fool could do. Only a fool would try.

As I crawled inside the culvert on my hands and knees, I kept asking myself why *I* was doing this, and also why Soup was not. I was hoping Soup would start creating a diversion, whatever that was, but all he did was bang on the iron of the culvert's rim with a stick and yell. He made one heck of a racket. The turkey turned his back to Soup, faced me, and stood his ground with yellow feet. Nothing else about him looked very yellow. I bet this old guy weighed close to thirty pounds.

"Here goes," I said.

Well, it all proves at least one thing. People (or turkeys) can look ferocious; but when the chips are down, lots of times they're just as afraid as you are. Pretending I was a dog, I gave a lunge at the turkey as well as a loud and healthy *woof*. I've always been able to bark pretty doggone well. My bark is much worse than my bite, even outdoors. But inside a dark culvert, my bark is sensational. It darn near ruptured my own eardrums. Would it scare a thirty pound turkey? As a matter of record, yes.

So much so that even Soup was caught totally unprepared. The turkey, upon viewing my rush and hearing my bark, turned tail to me and headed in the other direction. Right smack into Soup's arms!

"Grab him, Soup!"

Standing up to run, my head went *thud* into the roof of the culvert and half the canaries of the universe tweeted and twirped, and sang out little silver and gold stars, comets, and planets in the darkness. Stumbling forward, I fell on the turkey. Soup was on the bottom of the hogpile for once in his lucky life. I heard him grunt, either Soup or the turkey. That bird could kick like a mad mule. If he had on horseshoes, that old turkey couldn't have bucked any harder.

"Hold him, Soup. Hold him!"

I had a good purchase on the turkey's neck with both hands. I thought it was his neck until I discovered it was really Soup's. No wonder Soup was so quiet. I was half choking him to death. So I let loose and grabbed another neck, this one being a bit more feathery.

"We got him!" said Soup.

"Hang on," I said. "Grab his other leg."

Just in case you get asked, it sure is fun to chase a turkey. But to tell you the truth, it really isn't a whole lot of fun to catch it. That old bird could kick, scratch, and peck off a bulldog. Two bulldogs, as that was how determined Soup and I were to hang on.

"We really got him, Rob."

"Yeah, and he's got us," I croaked, just as a wing cracked across the bridge of my nose. A nose is sort of a sensitive place, especially *my* nose; and when a nose gets whacked by a turkey wing, it sure gets your attention. I was crying. Not a good old boo-hoo kind of a cry, but my eyes sure did fill up with tears. But then I forgot about my nose and started to think a great deal about my stomach, as that was where the turkey was kicking me.

"I got his leg," yelled out Soup.

"No! You got my finger. Let go!"

My mouth was full of feathers and not a single one tasted too good. But if that turkey had a sorry taste, it smelled even worse. The old bird must have got excited or something, because my nose was suddenly hit with worse than a wing. What a stench!

"Soup," I spat out a feather as I spoke, "I think this turkey has to go to the bathroom."

"He already has," said Soup, pinching his own nostrils.

"Maybe he's sick."

"If he ain't, I am," said Soup.

"Me too. I want to throw up."

"It's my turn first," said Soup, and he really started to gag. But I wasn't going to let old Soup be first at everything. So while he was still gagging, I really *did* throw up. I beat him. It made me happy in a sick sort of way.

The three of us gave up the struggle at once, and not one of our foul-smelling trio even had the gumption to get up. Nobody won. We all lost.

"Let's let him go," said Soup.

"Okay by me," I said. "We can't honestly say he's *ours*, or lay claim to any part of him."

"He belongs to that turkey farm," said Soup.

"By rights, we stole him."

"Over there is Ally Tidwell's house," said Soup.

"What about it?"

"His pa is a drunk."

"Everybody knows that," I said.

"Just made me ponder if all those Tidwells will have a turkey for Thanksgiving," said Soup.

"Sure they will."

"Last year," said Soup, "they had baloney for Thanksgiving dinner. Honest."

"How do you know that, Soup?"

"Ally told me. Besides the baloney he said they had macaroni and cheese."

"And no turkey?"

"No," said Soup. "It's sort of sad in a way. At our house, we always stuff a turkey or a big capon."

"So do we."

"I got an idea," said Soup.

"You don't even have to tell me," I said.

When I got home that day, in the late afternoon, I did my chores and then went into the house and told Mama and Aunt Carrie why I looked so tore up and smelled so sour. They heard the whole story, and at first it made them laugh a lot. But when I told about why we took the turkey to Mrs. Tidwell (who had too many kids, according to Aunt Matty) both my mother and Aunt Carrie stopped laughing. They became real quiet when I got to the part about the baloney.

I told them the truth. I told them how Soup and I promised each other that we'd work jobs on Saturday, and then walk all the way back to pay the turkey farmer whatever he said the old bird was worth. But then they made me take a bath, with soap, even though we weren't going for our usual Saturday night to do the town.

Later, they both came up to hug me goodnight.

"Do you reckon the Tidwells will be thankful when it comes to be Thanksgiving?" I asked my mother.

"Yes, they'll be right thankful," she said. "And so will I."

7

A Christmas Bell

"I got one," said Soup.

"And I just got two, stuck together."

Our mouths were wide open, eyes squinting upward to catch the snowflakes falling from an inky-blue December sky. White freckles on the face of Heaven.

"Hey look, Rob."

I looked to see a tiny star of snow quickly melt on the flat of Soup's tongue. White on red, like it was a frosty tidbit of winter. My mouth caught another snowflake, and a second later I gulped down the single drop of cool water. It even tasted like Christmas.

"Sure gets dark early this time of year," I said to Soup, as we walked along Main Street. We were each carrying a package, the present we got from the Christmas party at school. Every year we would exchange names, and then you earned a dime to buy a present for the kid whose name you drew. I drew Soup's name, and he really liked the "Big Little Book" that I'd carefully selected and wrapped with paper and string. His face lit up like a candle when he opened it at school, an hour ago, and saw it was *The Desert Eagle and the Hidden Fortress* by James O. Parsons.

"Whose name did you get, Soup?"

"Janice Riker."

"What'd ya give her? Poison, I hope."

"Naw," said Soup. "I figured what the heck, as long as it's Christmas and all, let bygones be bygones, so I got an emblem for her football helmet."

"I got a picture of Buck Jones."

"Yeah, I saw it," said Soup. "You must have showed it to me a hundred times."

A week ago, Miss Kelly had said that in her opinion it was best not to tell whose name you drew. I wanted to draw Norma Jean Bissell's name, so I could buy her a present that would silently proclaim, now and forever more, my dedicated devotion. I was sort of disappointed when I unfolded the tiny scrap of paper and (instead of her name) I read Luther Vinson. But I was glad that Soup liked the book. It was securely jammed deep into the pocket of his plaid coat.

"Come on," said Soup. "Why are you stopping?"

"I want to see Buck's picture again."

"You already looked at it a million times. At this rate," said Soup, "we'll never get to the courthouse."

"Hiya, Buck. Sure we will. It's just down the street." With tenderness due such a treasure, I stuffed Buck Jones back into his envelope.

Under our boots, the snow was packed where many feet had passed. The fresh snow sounded like music with every step, as though each snowflake was a note in a Christmas carol.

"Hurry up," said Soup. His fists were on his hips again. Best I hurry.

"Are you sure you pushed the note far enough under her door?" asked Soup. "Unless she reads the note, all our business at the courthouse won't amount to beans."

"I'm sure. Just before you gave her door knocker a rap, I made certain she'd find our message, so she'd listen at five o'clock."

"What did your note say again?"

"Dear Miss Kelly," I said to Soup. "Thanks for the swell party you gave us. We both had a nice time. But we all got stuff and you didn't get anything. So when you hear a bell ring at five o'clock, it is your Christmas present."

"Good," said Soup.

"I didn't sign our names, so she'll never know who it's from."

"You know, Rob, our first idea wasn't so hot."

"You're right. Miss Kelly probably wouldn't want your 'Big Little Book' or my autographed picture of Buck."

"If we had money, we'd *buy* her a present."

"If," I said. "We don't own a penny."

"Yeah, but if I know Miss Kelly," said Soup, "hearing us ring the old courthouse bell will be just as good a Christmas present. Maybe even better."

"She said once that money can't buy what people really want," I said. "And from the looks of *her* house, she's not too rich herself. Maybe she's sort of poor. Her front door needs a paint job."

"I guess Miss Kelly lives all alone in that little old place," said Soup.

"Did you look in her window?"

"Sort of," said Soup.

"I bet she didn't even have a Christmas tree."

"Didn't see one," Soup shrugged his shoulders.

"There's a clock in the dry goods store. It says quarter to five."

"We'd better hurry."

Christmas music was playing on Main Street. The town courthouse stood just south of the village green, an all-white building, structured as sturdy as a Methodist hymn. Everybody always said that our courthouse was so proud an edifice that it was indeed the outstanding feature of our community. Like the steeple on a house of worship, the belltower rose above the forward peak of the roof, a spire of Vermont justice. We ran through the new snow to the rear of the courthouse. Holding my pal Soup on my shoulders, I leaned against the wall as Soup tried to pry open a window. I heard it slide up.

"That was a leadpipe cinch," said Soup, scrambling

through the open window. Reaching out an arm, he helped to haul me inside. The sill hurt my stomach.

"Soup?" My voice was an echo. "Where do you think we are?"

"Looks like sort of an office. Come on, let's go through the main courtroom and into the front hall."

"Suppose we get caught?"

"We won't," whispered Soup.

"How do *you* know?"

"After we ring the bell, we'll hightail it to the back of the courthouse and outside through the same window. We'll leave it open."

"Yeah, but people will come running to see who rang the bell," I said. "They'll catch us for sure and certain."

"No, they won't. Because as they run to the *front* door, you and me'll just scoot out the back window, easy as pie."

Taking a deep breath, I let out a long sigh. I sure hoped Soup was right. It would be a downright shame to get caught in a mess of trouble just three days before Christmas. Especially when I wanted a genuine Red Ryder B-B gun so much, even though I knew the slim chances of receiving such a weapon as a gift from Mama or Aunt Carrie or even Aunt Matty.

"Soup?"

"Now what?"

"Don't you think we shoulda brought a flashlight or something to see with?"

"Nah. We don't need a flashlight."

"It's kind of dark in here." I cracked my knee against some hard thing that felt like a railing.

"You ain't scared, are ya?" asked Soup.

"Me scared? Don't be dumb."

The main courtroom was pitch dark. But each time a car would drive slowly by through the falling snow outside, its headlights cast spooky shadows on the gray walls and even up on the ceiling. I wanted to be somewhere else.

"Soup?" My voice sounded like a ghost.

"Come on, it's near to five o'clock."

"Okay, let's find the rope."

Silently we moved forward through the darkness, passing row after row of seats. They were sort of benches, like pews in a church. I was hoping nobody was in this big old place except for Soup and me. And to tell the straight of it, I was even hoping we wouldn't be here too long. Finally, we got to the front door at the rear of the courtroom. Soup tried the knob.

"It's locked," said Soup.

"Well, that settles it. Let's get out of here."

"Maybe," said Soup, "it isn't locked. Could be it's only stuck."

"What'll we do."

"Get in back of me," said Soup, "and grab your arms around my waist."

"Okay."

"Now pull," grunted Soup.

"I'm pulling, I'm pulling."

"Harder!"

"Hey, it came loose."

I never heard a squeakier-sounding door. The flesh on my backbone crawled around like my shirt was a sackful of snakes. As old Soup opened that door, it really gave me the creeps. That door was as high as a tree.

"Now," said Soup, "all we gotta do is find the bell rope."

"There it is," I said. And there it was; the end of the rope was about seven feet off the ground. Soup jumped up, but his hand didn't even come close.

"Maybe if I stand on your back," said Soup.

It didn't work. Soup tried getting up on my back, with no result, and then I tried getting up on his, but he wobbled a lot.

"Must be five o'clock by now," I said.

Soup nodded to me in the dark. "Yeah, and best we conjure up a way to ring that old bell, or Miss Kelly won't have a Christmas present. We gotta get up in the tower."

"Look," I said, "there's a ladder."

Sure enough, a long ladder leaned against the inside wall. Neither Soup nor I had noticed it at first, but now our eyes were becoming as accustomed to the surrounding nightlife as a pair of alley cats.

"Wow," said Soup in a hushed voice. "That sure is one heck of a long ladder. I can't even see up to the top rung. Can you, Rob?"

"No. It must reach all the way up to Heaven."

"We'll be able to reach that old rope easy from up there," said Soup. He put his foot on the first rung and started to climb. The ladder was near to straight up and tall.

"Soup?"

"Come on."

"Where does it go?"

"Up."

Fortified with Soup's learned explanation, I took a deep breath and started up. All I could see was the bottom of Soup's black overshoes. On each black heel was a tiny red ball. Here I go, I thought, messing up my Christmas by getting in trouble with Soup. It would take a miracle to get the B-B gun now.

Up climbed Soup. I followed. Just once I twisted my head over my shoulder to look down into the darkness at the dark floor of the courthouse below. I really didn't want to go any higher.

"Just remember," came a hollow voice from above. Soup's.

"Remember what?"

"We're doing this for Miss Kelly. She likes bells at Christmas, so bells she'll get. It's sort of like we're angels."

"Angels? Well, we're high enough to be."

"Don't make me giggle," said Soup. "I'm almost up to the top."

"Thank gosh," I whispered softly.

"What?"

"Nothing. Just don't change your mind and start coming down. If you do, you'll stomp on my fingers and make me fall."

"I won't. Rob?"

"Yeah?"

"Did you take your mittens off?"

"No. Did you?"

"Yes. It gives you a better purchase on the rungs of the ladder. Better do it."

"Up *here?*"

"Don't shout. You can hang on with one hand and pull the other mitten off with your teeth."

"Is that how you took yours off?"

"Yep, that's how," said Soup.

"Okay, I'll try it."

Between my teeth, my right mitten tasted sort of gritty. I wanted to gag. Yet, tug by tug, I yanked off my green mitten, removed it from my mouth with my bare hand, and stuffed it into my pocket, making sure not to crush a new, autographed glossy three-by-five photograph of my Hollywood hero. Teeth yanking, I jerked off the second mitten and dropped it. My left mitten landed with a soft wet *plop* on the wooden planks below me in the dark. So far below, I didn't want to even look down to see it.

"Soup?"

"You dropped it."

"I'm sorry. Best I go down and get it."

"You want to go *now?*"

"Yes. My mother said if I lose one more mitten I won't go sled riding or anything all winter long. And I probably won't get a Red Ryder either."

"Sure, you will," said Soup.

I'll say one thing for Soup, he was no pessimist. His presence was a warm and welcome sunbeam to pierce the dark of winter with raptured rays of confidence. He was rarely saddened by circumstance and was almost always as happy as a fiddle.

"We're awful high, Soup."

"You're telling me. Wait'll you get up *here*."

"Is it real high up?"

"I can hear a harp," laughed Soup. "Hey! I'm all the way up. There's a platform up here."

"Is there room for me?"

"Rob, old pal, there's always room for you."

Soup was right. The top of the ladder ended at a narrow platform. Reaching it, it took all the gumption I could muster to leave hold of the ladder and crawl onto what appeared to be sort of a shelf. My unmittened hands clung to the raw wood for dear life.

"Now what?"

"Now," said Soup, "we ring the bell."

"I can't see it."

"Neither can I, but it's gotta be up there somewhere."

Our four eyes strained upward into the darkness. Gradually I could make out a big circle, with a shiny spot in the middle. It was the *bell!* Its big black mouth looked like a monster coming down from the black roof,

ready to swallow up bad little boys who sneak into court-
houses.

"Golly!" said Soup.

"Sure is big. What if it falls on us?"

"It can't. Now all we have to do is lean out and grab
the rope."

"Lean *out?*" I looked down into a pit of what appeared
to be bottomless space. My hands were starting to get
wet. In fact, I sort of felt wet all over. Some of it was
snow that Eddy Tacker and Janice Riker had stuffed
down the back of my neck; yet the wet I felt wasn't all
due to a hunk of melted winter.

"Maybe I can reach the rope," said Soup, his hand
swinging out into the unlighted space. Boy, what a
drop. Well, I might as well try, too. My arm swung out
in an effort to grab the bell rope. That was when Soup
lost his balance, falling forward onto my back. One of
his legs slipped and hung out into space. I closed my
eyes. My heart stopped. And then my underpants suddenly became warm and wet. Soup kicked his leg to
keep from falling.

Over went the ladder!

Imagine an empty Vermont courthouse, boarded up
and barren of almost every comfort except wooden walls
and hard benches, crisp with cold, silent in the dark of
a December afternoon. When the ladder hit in that
hardwood floor, it produced a *bang* that my ears will
continue to hear if I live to be a hundred. It fell through

the tall door. What little liquid still remained hiding in my uncontrolled bladder suddenly exited into what was now a less-than-absorbent BVD.

"Oh, no!" I heard Soup say as he looked down.

"The ladder fell."

"Yeah, and I almost went with it."

"And me, too."

"Rob, we're trapped."

"How'll we get down?"

"Jump?" asked Soup.

"I think I'm going to be sick."

"You're right. We're up too high."

"I wouldn't jump down into there for all the money in the world. Not even for a dollar. I'd rather stay up here for the rest of my whole life."

"We just might," said Soup. "Or we could try to jump so we'd land on your mitten."

I couldn't laugh. It was just too scary up here in this dark old place with no way to get down.

"And we can't even ring the bell," I said.

"Miss Kelly won't get her present. And it'll be Christmas soon and maybe she won't get anything from anybody." Soup's voice was sort of odd.

"Soup, are you crying?"

"No," he said. But I knew he was.

"It's okay, Soup. The ladder wasn't your fault. You were only trying to reach the pullrope so's we could ring that big old bell."

"I messed it all up, Rob."

"No, you didn't. Why, we wouldn't even have got *this* far if it wasn't for you."

I could hear Soup crying. "Ya know," he said, choking back his sobs, "what makes me feel bad is that Miss Kelly will be waiting to hear a Christmas bell ring and it won't happen. She'll be all heartbroken, and she doesn't deserve to be let down. She's a real good lady."

"Maybe we can yell out a window, Soup. I remember there's windows near the bell. We can holler out. Somebody's bound to hear us."

A window was at our backs and open a crack. So we hollered. Then we listened. All we could hear was the Christmas music that some store was playing down below on Main Street. We yelled again, but as the echo faded off, we knew only an empty boarded up courthouse heard our cries.

"Help!" we yelled. Nobody answered. And I suddenly felt very cold.

We sat up on that wooden ledge, high up in a bell-tower, and thought. But I couldn't think of a way to ring the bell. Because we had no way. We just sat beside each other in the dark for a long, long time.

"I'm cold, Soup."

"Me too. My teeth are chattering. But I found the answer to our problem."

"You did?"

"If it'll work. Our ledge goes all the way around."

"Tell me, Soup. What's the answer?"

"We reach that rope," said Soup, "by making a rope."

"Making a rope? How?"

"With our clothes," said Soup.

We did it.

Taking off our coats and shirts and finally our pants, we tied them together so that Soup could stand on one side of the bell rope and throw the rope of clothes over to me to the other side of the ledge. Then we walked back to the same wall of the tower, and the rope came with us, carried to where we could reach it by our rope of clothes. Hanging on to the bell rope, we finally loosened the knots from our clothing. I was so cold and my body was shaking so hard, I didn't think I'd ever get dressed. I felt like an icicle.

"Now," said Soup, "we can ring that old bell for Miss Kelly's Christmas."

"Good," I said. "Let's pull."

Pull we did. But the rope was too heavy and the bell didn't swing on its axle quite far enough to ring. And once we almost pulled ourselves over the edge. My hands were gripping that rope like the talons of a hawk. Yet we couldn't get the bell to swing against its clapper. Not even one little brassy tinkle.

"I give up," said Soup. His voice was quiet, sounding as if he was really defeated for the first time in his life. In disgust, he dropped the rope. So did I. And then the two of us looked at each other.

"Maybe we coulda slid down the rope," said Soup.

"My hands couldn't hold me," I said, "not after all

that pulling and tugging. My fingers are so weak and cold, I'd let loose."

"Yeah," said Soup, "and we'd fall to death."

"We'll never get down," I said, "never."

"Is this old courthouse closed up all winter long, Rob?"

"Reckon it is. Our town is the county seat, but I don't guess they all have much to sit about in winter."

"And nobody knows we're here," said Soup.

"We're just failures," I said. "We get an F for bell-ringing."

Again we tried yelling as loud as we could yelp, but I guess the music down on Main Street was too noisy to let any passer-by hear us.

"Rob, we could be here all night."

"And freeze to death. Last night it was below zero, or so Aunt Carrie said."

"I'm cold already," said Soup.

"And I'm hungry. We were due home an hour ago for chores. Even if I don't freeze to death, Mama and Aunt Carrie will kill me for being so late. And not even showing up for supper."

"They don't know where we are, Rob."

We sat on the wooden ledge of the belltower, as close to each other as we could get, trying to keep warm. It sure was a mistake when we'd taken our clothes off. Even though we were now fully dressed again, it was sort of like my blood had stopped circulating. I sure wished I had my other green mitten. I was so cold, so very,

very cold. And I couldn't stop my body from shaking, like the way you sometimes get crying and can't make yourself stop.

Suddenly, a light.

Not much of a light, but down below us in the blackness of the empty courthouse, a tiny flash of light was coming along the floor. Somebody was down there. Now we'd get caught and get ourselves punished. But then we heard a voice! Not a stranger, but the voice that both Soup and I knew well, a voice that represented much in our world that stood for courage and truth and everything else that was righteous. A voice out of breath from hurry.

It was Miss Kelly.

"Boys, are you in here? Robert? Luther?"

"Miss Kelly," I said, "you *came*."

"Where are you?" Miss Kelly's light was searching all over the floor of the courthouse, finding no one. Then it stopped on my one fallen mitten.

"We're up here," yelled Soup. His voice sounded sort of weak and cold.

Quickly we saw the tiny pinpoint of her flashlight grow sharper, and we were in the circle of its light. We waved down to Miss Kelly. "Up here," I said, "and we can't get down."

"We came to ring the bell," said Soup.

"I know," said Miss Kelly. "And when I heard no bell, I wondered why. I had to figure out which bell and where. It took me too long, I suppose, to conclude that there had to be a very serious reason why a bell *didn't* ring."

"We knocked over the ladder," I said.

"It wasn't Rob, Miss Kelly," said Soup. "I knocked over the ladder."

"Here it is," said Miss Kelly. "I found the ladder. Now if I can raise it."

I don't know how she did it, but she did. Miss Kelly got that ladder up quicker than scat. Wrong place at first, but then Soup and I grabbed the top and got it steadied against the edge of the platform.

"Just don't fall," Miss Kelly yelled up to us.

We got down. I got my mitten.

"How did you get in, Miss Kelly?" asked Soup.

"When I saw the open window, it told me all I needed to know," she said. "I got in, I presume, the same way you did."

"We wanted to give you a gift," I said, "for Christmas."

"Because you didn't get a present," said Soup.

Miss Kelly was down on her knees, so she could put an arm around Soup and one around me. She held our faces close to hers. She kissed each one of us on the cheek, not saying anything, just biting her lower lip. Her chin was trembling. I guess because she was cold. All she had on was her big gray sweater.

"How did you know it was the two of *us*, Miss Kelly. I never signed our names to the note."

"I knew," she said. "And then the silence told me to

come fetch you. At first I thought you were playing a joke. But when there was no bell . . ."

Soup said, "You must know a lot about bells, Miss Kelly."

"And about boys," she said. She still hung onto us very hard. "When they're bad and when they're beautiful."

We tried the front door. It was locked. Then laughing, the three of us went out through the back window and through the snow to Miss Kelly's house where we had cookies and hot cocoa. Then we ran for home.

"Merry Christmas, Miss Kelly!" we yelled back to her as she stood in the doorway, waving to us as we ran through the snow. She was holding my note close to her throat.

On the way home, the new snow made music under our boots. I said to Soup, "Gee, I wish we'd given a Christmas gift to Miss Kelly."

"Rob," said Soup, "I got a hunch we did."

Soup and its popular sequels portray the adventures of Robert Newton Peck's childhood, and like all his books, are deeply rooted in the Vermont country where he grew up. His highly acclaimed first novel, A *Day No Pigs Would Die*, is about his own family and boyhood on a Vermont farm. *Millie's Boy*, his second novel, has the vernacular humor and directness characteristic of the region. *Path of Hunters*, a story of animal struggle in a meadow, is based on the author's early and continuing observations of nature.